A Promise Kept

E lei kau, e lei hoʻoilo i ke aloha.

Love is worn like a lei (wreath) through the summers and winters.

Love is everlasting—a Hawaiian proverb

Published in Great Britain 2003 by

MASTERWORKS INTERNATIONAL
27 Old Gloucester Street
London
WC1N 3XX
England

Tel: 0780 3173272
Email: books@masterworksinternational.com
Web: http://www.masterworksinternational.com

ISBN: 0-9544450-1-5

Artwork by Morag Campbell

Cover Photograph of Kauai's South Shore
by Phil Young

ACKNOWLEDGEMENTS

This is not a work of fiction but the characters names and some locations have been changed.

I am indebted to the following people; Arnë, for without him the whole experience would not have unfolded, Bhagwant Singh Khalsa for his continuing enthusiasm for proof reading my writings, and Brenda Turville of Kapa'a, Kaua'i for her support and help in getting Malia Rogers and Aunty Sarah Sheldon, also of the Hawaiian island of Kaua'i, to translate the chant at the end of A Promise Kept into the Hawaiian language. Hopefully, all the 'okina and macrons are in the right place. A big thank you goes to Kiri and T'hane.

Morag Campbell is a writer, poet, teacher, healer and nature mystic who lives in England.

To honour Kiri's wish that his teachings be passed on to as wide an audience as possible we invite you to visit the MasterWorks International website where you can find out how you can learn more about the Kahuna teachings.

www.masterworksinternational.com/huna

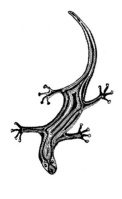

How do I know thee
Have we met before
I seem to know you
But am yet unsure

How do I know
With every fibre of my being
That though the face is unknown
It is you that I am seeing

How can I tell
Through eons of time
That I have always been yours
And you mine

How do I love Thee
For I know that I do
For life after life
I have loved only you

How do I know
With steps unsure
That the two of us
Have walked this way before

How do I know
What makes me say
That you and I
go back a long way

How do I know
As I look in your face
That our love has transcended
All time and all space

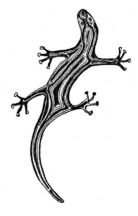

How do I know
It's enough that I do
And for this moment in time
I'm united with you

ONE FINE DAY

 My head ached from the sheer effort of forcing the air in and out of my lungs. The back of my neck felt like iron and I was having trouble focusing my eyes on the page in front of me. Fortunately the shop was quiet. A young girl with a spangled top sat crossed legged on the floor bathing in the shaft of sunlight that streamed through the courtyard window. Shining specks of dust whirled around her. They drifted slowly down to alight on her head and shoulders only to be hurled upward again as she periodically shifted the weight on her buttocks as the hard wooden floor took its toll on her musculature. Her head was bowed reverently into the book she was reading. I doubted that she would buy it but I enjoyed the sight of her and so right now that didn't really matter that much.

Further back, over to the left of the calligraphy sets and Tai Chi figures in the section on metaphysics, stood a distinguished looking man. I guessed that he would be in his fifties. He wore a dark grey suit. His slightly portly figure conveyed an air of contentment and quiet authority. I had seen him in the shop many times. Sometimes he would buy, sometimes he would just give the rows of books a cursory glance and spend most of time staring at me in a kind of soft, defocused way when he thought I wasn't aware. I had over the years perfected the art of watching customers with my peripheral vision whilst appearing to be engrossed in some book or paperwork, an art developed by most bookshop keepers, I suspect, especially those not affluent enough to have the array of video cameras and convex mirrors of the bigger stores. When I went into surveillance mode I would sometimes catch his dreamy look in my direction. It was a bit disconcerting but I paid it no real attention. There were some times when he just seemed to pop in for the briefest of visits and on those occasions would pass the time of day or ask if I could acquire a certain book for him. He was kind of spooky I decided. Not in a queer way. It was just that I didn't seem to be able to quite get the measure of him.

Just as I had suspected, the girl rose from her crossed legged position and slowly placed the book she was reading back on the self. She turned towards my desk by the door as she moved to leave.

"No good?" I inquired.

"No, not really," she replied, "I was looking for inspiration I guess."

She was looking for inspiration! God, what wouldn't I give for inspiration right now! A good deep breath would be heaven. She smiled sweetly and I forgave her for not purchasing the book. Anyway I hadn't the energy to argue with myself about whether I should be upset about my store being used as a resource centre. I wanted to close up. It was already mid afternoon and business was slow. Who wants to be browsing a bookshop on a great sunny day like today! However, I couldn't very well ask the man to leave so I stood up and picked up the small pile of books that had been delivered earlier. I had finished logging them and moved to place them on the shelves. From somewhere in the middle of my chest a small whistle escaped. At first I wasn't sure if I had really heard it or even if it was really me. Even though I heard it regularly as the asthma took hold, I was surprised and dismayed every time. I just knew I was in for a long night.

I decided the books could wait and sat down again. The leather seat sighed beneath me in sympathy with my mood. Without thinking, I rested my head in my hands, elevating my shoulders to make my breathing easier. I closed my eyes and prayed. Dear God, what do I have to do to get rid of this? Ten years of this was more than enough for anyone. As I dragged my hands down and away from my face and began to re-focus, I found myself staring at the buckle of a belt which was hovering right in front of my face. I hadn't even heard the man move. Drawing back my attention and lifting my gaze. I looked into the man's distinguished face. It was quite rounded and the skin was well tanned. Streaks of grey hair at his temples accentuated his face. His steel grey eyes were locked firmly on me. They seemed kindly enough in a penetrating way, but they never left my face for a moment.

"Yes, can I help you," I breathed.

"On the contrary," he said, "can I help you? When are you going to do something about that chest of yours?"

His voice was soft and low and seemed to come from somewhere in the centre of his thorax.

"Come and see me," he said.

He turned, his face giving away nothing, and walked out of the shop.

When I managed to drag my eyes away from the imprint of his form in the doorway, I noticed the card on top of the pile of books.

It was plain white with an ornate but finely executed border in black ink. It merely said:

'Arnë Peters, BioSynthesis Institute' and a telephone number.

I locked up the shop and with painful effort and slow steps made my way back to the house. Fortunately, I did not have far to go, but even so, I felt so exhausted when I eventually arrived that I just fell into the settee and stayed there, not even attempting the few steps to my bedroom. As I had known, the night was an eternity—a marathon of laboured breathing and sharp pains in my head and chest. The tedium was broken only by the bouts of coughing as my poor body tried to clear my lungs of mucus. The morning found me exhausted and pale and desperate. There was no way that I could open the shop today.

I called Marge, the girl who ran the health shop across the way from the bookshop and asked her to open up and keep an eye on the place for me. It was going to be another hot day and neither one of us was expecting a lot of business. She agreed. It made her feel good to think she was helping and she knew that I would return the favour when I could. Besides, I had been aware for some time that she was attracted to me and she would see this as a way of currying favour. Was that bad of me? Shit, I didn't have the energy to care. I made myself a hot tea and fell into a deep sleep.

The cave was damp and rancid smelling. Small rivulets of water ran down the walls and formed a larger stream on either side of the pathway. I had to stretch out my arms on either side to place the palms of my hands on the slimy surface so that I could blindly find my way towards the small glow of yellow light somewhere off to my right. My feet slid, rather than walked, along the mud floor and my lungs were having a hard time extracting the oxygen from the dank air. I was shuffling like an old man and my shoulders ached from the effort of keeping my arms stretched out to the side. Stabbing pains shot periodically across my back and chest, radiating like meteor bursts from below my scapulas. Something in me told me I had to keep going. I had to get out of this place. The passage way opened up into a bigger, although not what you would call spacious, area with a smooth rock floor. A huge stalagmite rose from the centre of the space to almost touch the roof of the cave. It glistened in the light of the torch burning in its holder on the wall. My legs were shaking from the effort of the descent and my head was swimming from lack of oxygen. I stumbled,

10

and as the floor rushed to meet me I could feel myself blacking out. After a time, from somewhere in the darkness, I could feel warm hands on my chest and a warm, deep voice, whispered;

"Go inside little one. Deep, deep down inside yourself. That's right... Down and down. Deeper and deeper. Oh little one, you are one of life's treasures are you not? And treasures are kept in a chest. A chest full of treasures which only you can open. Treasurers beyond your wildest dreaming... deep, deep down inside your treasure chest. That's right... deep inside. All these treasures, hidden deep in this treasure chest of yours can be yours if only you would reach down... down inside. That's right... Just keep abreast of things and all things will come to you. Now, reach down and just open up the chest... that's right... open it up. That's right. Now, open it up some more... good; and more still. Now let it open wide. Now breath deep, breathe down further and further into the chest of treasures, breathe all the way down and you will come up free."

The voice sounded vaguely familiar.

It was early evening when I eventually awoke. The phone was ringing.

"Hi there," said Marge. "How are you feeling?"

Truth to tell I was suddenly feeling a lot better. My body felt weak but easier, like I had just come out of a fever.

"Not bad," I said. "How did it go today? Not too busy I hope."

"No, no. I sold a couple of books and one of the porcelain dragons and a set of the handmade paper by the till. You know the ones with the little speckles of red in. That's it."

"Thanks Marge," I mumbled. "I'm grateful. See you tomorrow."

I could tell she wanted to talk but I replaced the receiver

before she could say more. I was ravenously hungry.

That night I slept well. There was the usual mumbo jumbo of dreams that, try as I might to recall the next morning, eluded me in the tantalising way that dreams do. But I paid them no real mind and was in a particularly good mood as I drew up the blinds on the shop window and wedged open the door ready for business. There was no sign of Marge as yet. She pretty much kept her own hours, opening late often and disappearing in the mid afternoon more often than not. It was no way to run a business but it was no concern of mine and I set to tidying the shelves. The first couple of hours after opening were, I decided, the best of the day. People never seemed to drift in much before 10.30 a.m. and it gave me the chance to go about the morning meditation of dusting, tidying and sometimes reading.

The day proved fruitful. There was not a large number of customers that day and the usual number of floaters, you know the ones that just drift in, waft around the room trance like, and drift out again, but those that found something of interest to keep them there were willing to part with their money and by the close of day I was well pleased. As I was pulling down the blind on the front window, the girl from a couple of days ago walked past. She caught my eye and smiled a little. I watched her walk on down the road. She was tall and moved well. Today she was wearing red slacks and a check blouse. Over her shoulder was a large brown bag. She was walking purposefully, her blond hair bobbing as she walked. I found myself staring at her back, mesmerized by the roll of her hips in the tight slacks. My hand was poised on the blind.

"Hey Hugh, do you fancy a coffee before home?"

The voice startled me and I spun around ridiculously almost losing my balance. I had answered before thinking and five minutes later saw Marge and I walking towards the wine bar on the High street. Over my first cappuccino I quickly began to regret the decision and by half way through the second I could feel the hooks in my back and I was landed. I kicked myself all the way home. Why was I so spineless? Why couldn't I just say, Well Marge I like you a lot too but I don't want a relationship right now. I was still trying to extricate myself from my latest relationship disaster. Why didn't I get up and make an excuse to leave when she first suggested the idea of the date? Why? Why? By the time I got home I had run through every excuse in the book as to why I was unable to keep our appointment but when it came right down to it I knew that I had to go through with it. Hell, I saw her just about every day—better to just go and get it over with.

As it happened fate took a hand and on the appointed day of the dreaded date with Marge. I was flat on my back wrestling with my breath again and concluding that dying was as good a way of avoiding the encounter as any. Although I had been cursed with asthma for years, and believe me that's what it felt like—a curse, I had always vehemently refused to resort to an inhaler. I suppose I didn't want to become dependent on it and somewhere inside I had the inkling that I could actually beat it, but there was always a price to pay for my stubbornness. I managed to survive a long day, and an even longer night, and struggled into the shop the next morning, where I sprawled in a chair and tried not to glance too many times at my pale and sickly reflection in the window. Marge was nowhere to be seen for which I was grateful. At 11.45 a.m. I decided to close temporarily and go get an espresso. The excuse being that the theophylline in it would ease my breathing. Just as I was levering myself out of the chair, he walked in. He shot me a long hard stare. This time his gaze was not as friendly as it had been the day he left his card on my desk. I was suddenly and inexplicably overcome with guilt. I actually felt guilty that I had not phoned him to get some help with my chest! But hey, I argued, it had been fine for a few days and anyway it's not like I made him a promise or anything. He walked silently over to the shelves and began side-stepping along the row of books, his eyes darting over the titles.

From somewhere behind me, as I thought, I heard a voice say; "Uh, you know you said that you could help sort out my chest, well if you think you can help, how about we give it a go?"

It was only when he turned to face me and replied "Sure." that I realized that it had been me that had spoken.

We arranged to meet the following day in the morning.

"I'll come to your place," he said and turned and left.

Shit! I'd have to ask Marge to watch the shop again! It never occurred to me to wonder how the guy knew where to find me. I was renting a small apartment across the street from the shop and I suppose he must have seen me leave in the mornings to open the shop or meandering back there at the close of day. Anyway true to his word at 10.30am the next morning there he was on my doorstep. I felt apprehensive about showing him into the tiny lounge and we stood awkwardly for a few minutes. At least I stood awkwardly he, as always, looked self possessed and at ease.

"You sit there," he said gesturing towards the settee.

I did as I was told. He, on the other hand, pulled up a hard wooden chair from the corner of the room which he sat on the wrong way round so that he could rest his elbows on the chair back. As I sat tentatively on the settee my head and chest were in a vice. I lifted my arms to place one on the arm of the settee and the other along the back of it. To the casual observer it may have looked like I was sitting back and relaxing but I knew that if I propped up my shoulders it would lift my chest

14

and make breathing that tiny bit easier. Under Arnë's steady gaze, I was even more aware of my breathing than usual. I was puffing like a grampus, what ever that is. I remember asking myself the question as I listened to my chest whistling and squeaking every time I tried to draw some air into my lungs. The noise of my breathing filled the tiny room and magnified it out of all proportion so that the sound filled my head and I could feel myself panicking. It even seemed to be drowning out the sound of the traffic outside.

"Okay, Hugh," Arnë said in his deep warm voice, "I want you to sit back and relax and close your eyes. As you sit back and relax really focus on your breathing."

"No problem," I thought, "I've had no choice but to focus on it for hours."

Arnë continued.

"As you become aware of your breathing, notice also the noise of the air as it forces its way into your lungs and as you notice the sound become aware of the noise of the traffic outside the window. As you notice the sound of your breathing and the noise of the traffic you become aware of the feel of the settee as it supports you. That's right... and as you become aware of the noises and the feel of the settee you find yourself letting go a little and as you let go a little you find yourself sinking just a little into the settee. That's right. And as you allow yourself to relax some more you find yourself sinking deeper and deeper into the settee. Good. Notice also that your fingers are beginning to unclench and the more they unclench the easier your breathing becomes. In fact your breathing only gets easier and easier at the same rate as your fingers start to uncurl and your hand opens up on the arm of the settee."

Arnë's voice droned on. At one point I remember thinking, so this is hypnosis.

From a far away place I heard him say;

"You are walking through a fine meadow. The lush dark summer green grass, is soft and yielding beneath your feet and the sun is friendly and warm on your face. As you feel the sun on your face every tiny muscle in your body starts to relax into the warmth. Every so often there are trees dotted about the meadow. Birch trees, dainty and tall with silver white trunks gently wave as you pass by. Their branches hung with fine leaves that flash differing colours of green with the changing currents of air. The leaves rustle as the air passes over them, dancing and delighting in the air around them. You notice how the leaves shimmer and dance in the breeze and the light rustling sound that they make drifts across the grass to greet you. You approach an oak. Strong and powerful the great trunk pushes up from the earth to create a vast canopy of leaves, dark against the sky. The sunlight filters through the canopy and flickers across your face as you walk beneath it. It feels strong and protective. The air is slightly cooler here and you pause a moment beneath its green umbrella before moving on and out into the sunlight again. You notice that the heady, musty sweet smell of earth beneath the tree is replaced by the sharp, sweet smell of grass, crushed beneath your feet.

As you walk on across the meadow feeling light and easy, you notice ahead of you a small river. Sparkling silver flashes of light draw your eyes to it and you head towards it. As you reach its banks you are aware of being hot and sticky with the effort of walking and the heat of the sun. Your clothes feel suddenly uncomfortable and restrictive. You feel compelled to rid yourself from their clamminess. You look around. You are alone. Taking off your clothes you place them on a large nearby stone and watch the river running clearly in front of you. You can hear its merry chatter as it passes over the stones at the river's edge and you smell its freshness in the hot summer air. It is inviting. It calls to you. Calls to you to leave the river bank and your clothes which suddenly look old and worn and venture into the heart of its cool waters. You have no desire to take the clothes with you, they no longer feel right, no longer seem to fit you some how. Suddenly, a new smell assails your nostrils. The sweet smell of wood smoke. Looking

16

further down the river you see that someone has lit a fire. It is smouldering quietly, sending wisps of white smoke along the river bank. Picking up your clothes you walk toward the fire and, on impulse, throw them one by one on to the fire. It smokes, sending great clouds of white billowing around you. The fire gains strength quickly in the dry air, crackling and snapping in the air around you. Smoke climbs effortlessly into the air tracing lazy spirals above you, flames lick at the cloth and it succumbs to their attention, smouldering and blackening.

After a while, the fire has a hold and dances and plays before you, its heat adding to the suns rays and warming your body even more. You feel relieved and satisfied. You no longer need them after all. Turning to the river, you dip your toe in and feel the rush of the water and its cool, healing balm. Your whole body responds to its seductive pull and you step into the flowing water and make your way to the middle of the river. Sliding beneath the silky water you submerge your self for a moment. Beneath the water all is quiet. Breaking the surface you feel the wind adding its refreshing touch to your face and you walk across to the far bank. Drawing yourself out of the river you feel refreshed, renewed, different, cleansed. All of the old you has mysteriously and miraculously been washed away. You now feel stronger, more potent. Nothing can affect you now. You have a core of strength and resolve that is unassailable. Looking around you see, on a rock nearby, a fresh set of clothing. It is a new suit of clothing shimmering like spun silver. Slipping it on, you find it moulds and fits to your body perfectly. It reinforces the feeling of invincibility that now floods through you. It affirms the new you, a new you that is stronger, more powerfully in control yet calm and relaxed in your new identity. Feeling renewed you take a deep breath and revel in the surge of air flooding into your lungs and the rush of strength that accompanies it. You take another... and another. It is so easy. Far off to your right you hear a crow call a greeting and you walk powerfully and purposefully toward the sound, your feet travelling effortlessly over the grass, the wind in your face, breathing deeply."

I followed the instructions as long as I could until my mind kind of flipped out and although I was aware of his voice I was becoming less and less sure of what he was actually saying. There was something about my little finger and feeling invincible I remembered afterwards. The session seemed to end abruptly. One minute I was off I don't know where, and the next I was sitting in my settee staring at Arnë who was sitting in exactly the same position I had left him in when we started.

"Is that it?" I asked.

"Yes," he replied, "see how you feel and let me know. I'll be around. Don't get up. I'll see myself out."

I watched him cross the room and disappear around the corner into the hall. I didn't move until I heard the catch on the front door. I felt kind of weird. I looked down at my hands with their fingers spread wide across my thighs. I had no recollection of moving them. There was a kind of vibration in my body and I did feel extremely calm but best of all, my chest felt great! I took a giant breath and waited for the whistle. It never came. When I finally rose out of the chair I was feeling great. I felt strong and connected and at ease with myself. I remembered something about being invincible?

Well I wasn't convinced that it had anything to do with the session that I had received from Arnë but my life suddenly got a lot better. To be honest it had been a bit of struggle of late. The shop hadn't yet started to make me any real money as yet. I was living in a small flat and as usual my relationships sucked. I don't know why but when it came to women I was a complete basket case most of the time. I had always been extremely emotional. But at times, I was so completely overwhelmed by my emotions to the extent that I couldn't function half the time. To make matters worse, I always seemed to be attracted to the most neurotic women in the area.

I had slowly begun extricating myself from my last girlfriend. A process that always took time for me. The shop was becoming more viable. Then, surprisingly, a legacy from my fathers' estate, which had been tied up for years, due to a legal blunder, suddenly got resolved. This was down to my good fortune in finding a local solicitor who wasn't afraid of a fight. He had taken on the big boys and won! The upshot of which was that I suddenly found myself with a sizeable amount of money. There was no question as to what I should spend it on. I was feeling cramped in my present rented apartment and with my growing sense of omnipotence I decided I needed to buy a bigger house. I did the usual round of agents and looked at a wide variety of houses. Of course there was no shortage of advice and every day Marge had something to say on the matter, most of which revolved around what she liked in a house.

Hmm, she's getting ideas above her station, I remember musing one afternoon after yet another fruitless house visit followed by a tirade of unsolicited advice.

Then I found it! It was beautiful. A large, early Victorian house in a short terrace. The entrance hall was imposing so it caught me right from the start. A spiralling staircase took off from in front of you as you entered the hall and as you stood in the well of the house you could see it wending its way up four flights. It sucked you in. The lounge, off to the right of the stairway, was twice the size of my present accommodation with a huge bay window. The house was of that era when rooms had high ceilings and good proportions so the whole place had this wonderfully spacious feel. Through to the back was a smaller room with a window as well as a large room with side windows looking out onto a courtyard. Right at the back was a kitchen and utility room which finally lead out into a raised walled garden. Above this level were six more rooms and an attic. It was huge!

"What in the world do you want such a enormous house for Hugh?" Marge asked me the next day as I described the place to her. "There's only you for God's sake!"

"I don't care." I replied, "I want the house. It feels great and it reminds me of the house I grew up in. Besides maybe I'll think of some ways of utilising the extra space."

This last bit of conversation slipped out casually but it got me thinking. Maybe I should think of a way of making the most of all that space. I guess the thought was working away in my subconscious because what looked like a bizarre series of events then occurred.

For the last few years I had been travelling to the next city, one evening a week, to train in Tai Chi Chuan with a guy called Paolo. He was a very accomplished martial artist. As far as I could make out it was his life's work. Years of daily practice and study had made him accomplished in all the internal martial arts of Tai Chi, Pakua, and Hsing-I. He was also a natural with both sword and staff as well as the empty hand forms—a real inspiration. I got to be pretty friendly with him over time and I had even volunteered to act as guinea pig for his acupuncture training. It's traditional for martial artists to be accomplished in some kind of healing practice. It is something about having the skills to help your students if they got injured during practice! Paolo had chosen acupuncture in line with his Taoist lifestyle. For two years we would sit in a bar after the class and he would take my pulses, then later back at his place I'd get needled. At about the time that I bought the house he was about to qualify and needed a place to practice.

"Come to my place," I heard myself say, as I lay sprawled out on the floor of his place after class one night. "I've got loads of room. It would be easy enough to set one up as a treatment room for you."

So that's how the Tree of Life Healing Centre got started and I woke up one morning to find that I now had two businesses. Pretty soon as well as Paulo, Arnë came to work there and then a girl who did massage and a homeopath. Some time previous to this I had actually done a course in Jin Shin Do acupressure. But, strangely, it didn't feel totally right for me to practice it. I decided that as I had my very own healing centre it would make sense for me to train in some other kind of therapy that I felt I could offer. I also moved my own Tai Chi class that I had started some time ago in a local hall into the larger of the two rooms on the ground floor. The Tai Chi group provided an outlet for my latent teaching skills and I found the process of working with people's movement difficulties a real buzz.

There was one young guy in the group who was built like a stick insect but with none of the co-ordination. If he was concentrating on his arms his legs went all over the place. When he got his legs sorted his mind would fuse. He wore a stack of metal bracelets on one wrist and every time he moved they jangled. After a while they jangled me too. They had to come off! Another guy had done some Karate and was struggling with the adjustment from hard to soft. The women in the class were generally better than the men initially. They were already softer and more yielding with greater body awareness. There was one woman in particular who looked really promising. She was tall and slim with natural grace and an easy way of moving. It was hard to place her age. Streaks of grey hair framed her good looking face. She was older than me certainly, but not that much I thought. She was interesting I decided. Hey, what did I mean by that? Well she seemed a natural in the class and she was keen. She was probably the only student who had obviously practiced between classes, and believe me that was rare. There was something wistful and vulnerable about her. She could have been neurotic, as I said, I can usually pick them out at a glance, but I didn't think so. I'm really good at picking neurotic women, I just had to look back at my past girlfriends to verify that! She definitely looked fragile though and yes I admit it—I fancied her. The broad gold band on her ring finger warned me off however. Still she was attractive and I liked having her in the class.

It was the gangly, jangly Tai Chi student who, surprisingly, provided the answer as to which therapy I should train in. He came in with a book one evening on something called Polarity Therapy. The book didn't give much of a clue as to what it was about but he said that he had had some sessions and they were the best treatments he had ever received. I took the book home and the next unwitting friend who stopped by the Centre, found herself stretched out on the floor whilst I placed one hand on her head whilst the other rocked her abdomen. When I stopped the rocking the feeling in my hands was electric!

The next day I set about tracking down where I could learn more. Trainings in England, I found, had a difficult time structure for me. They were long and mostly took place over the weekends and of course Saturdays were frequently my most busy time in the book shop. I had to find another way of learning this system. Then I found an advertisement in the back of a Yoga magazine. It was for an intensive training, not long and drawn out like the one in England, so I could do it in one long time span. There was only one snag, the course was in San Francisco! On impulse, I telephoned the contact name at the back of the magazine. So what if the course was in San Francisco. Hell, I'd always wanted to visit there. I didn't take much persuading to sign up for the intensive training. The man I spoke to sounded committed and trustworthy and the whole thing felt like it would be some great adventure and it was a great excuse to visit the States, something I'd always dreamed about. It felt like now was the right time. On impulse one evening, I decided to consult the I-Ching about whether or not I should go and it said, 'the man has a gift, he should learn how to use it.' Divination doesn't come any clearer than that, so I seized the moment. I arranged for an old girlfriend to work in the shop whilst I was away and left the Tree of Life to run itself. Most of the therapists working there took their own bookings anyway and each had a key to the place so I figured that things would tick over smoothly there for the weeks that I would be away. I cancelled the Tai Chi class and flew out three weeks after my call to the States.

NOT OUT OF THE WOODS YET!

As luck would have it there was just myself and one other man taking the training which proved to be immensely satisfying. I booked into a small boarding house near the school on arrival, and whilst it was small and basic, it served me well enough. San Francisco was stunning. I loved the clarity of the light in the early mornings when the mists had cleared, the cosmopolitan feel to the place, the plethora of ethnic restaurants and the architecture. The whole area was composed of steep streets of row upon row of brightly coloured wooden doll's houses with stained glass doors. I would start the day with coffee and bagels at a nearby café and then start the long slow climb to the school from the small guest house which I had found to stay in for my time there. Even the steep streets, which are a feature of the city, didn't bring on my asthma and I was beginning to feel that the tide really had turned. My life was panning out pretty well. Here I was at twenty eight with two small, but reasonably successful, businesses and a developing healing gift that I never knew I had.

"Feel that," my instructor said to a colleague of his that had come to be a 'body' for me to practice on one day during the course. "Its like a light bulb going on isn't it?"

I don't know whether it was the years of Tai Chi or just a natural aptitude but the energy in my hands was intense. The more I worked with them the more vibrant they became. I still had a tendency to get over emotional about things, but right now I realized that in my present state everything was going well with just about everything in my life.

When I came back from the States I was full of enthusiasm over my new found abilities. I worked for two days a week at my Centre and the rest of the week was spent in the bookshop. My old flame, Tania, who had looked after the place whilst I was away was persuaded to stay on and cover for me when I was at the Centre. I couldn't rely on Marge to cover her place and mine on a regular basis. The presence of Tania in the shop had had an unexpected side affect. Marge had backed right off and was even a little cold towards me on my return. There wasn't even a suggestion of coffee never mind a date from her. I was relieved. It was always great when a situation sorted itself out without effort and as I have already mentioned, relationships aren't exactly my forte. When Arnë wasn't working at my place he also practiced at a couple of other venues, one of which was a small residential centre run by a doctor and his wife with the help of visiting therapists. Arnë suggested that I might like to do a day there also. The people who went there were mostly suffering from cancer and some of them were in a really bad state. He suggested that it would expand my experience and he thought that my 'hands on' approach to therapy would be of benefit to them. I decided to take a look at the place. Hey, what had I got to lose? So one bright summer morning I took off along the coast road to give a short talk on what I did to the residents.

The place, I discovered, was formerly a small seaside hotel and it still retained some of that energy. It was a detached Victorian house with a small neat garden in front displaying a large board which announced that it was the Park Centre for Complementary Therapy and that the director was a Dr Marcus O'Shea. It was built along with a row of similar houses at right angles to the sea front. There was no sea view but a short walk took you down and on to the shingle beach. The hotel, in its new life, had gained a colonic room where a large Teutonic looking woman in a white coat did unspeakable things with rubber tubing and water and two of the downstairs rooms next to the dining area were given over to therapy rooms, each sporting a bodywork table, desk and two chairs.

As I arrived, a small group of people had gathered in the lounge in anticipation of my talk. I didn't allow myself to get too carried away with this level of interest. I guessed there wasn't much entertainment to be had in a place like this and I was at least a change of face so I didn't kid myself that they were desperate to hear what I had to say. Then again maybe they were. I knew from Arnë that most of them had done the rounds of orthodox physicians and even tried most alternative therapies. Hope springs eternal they say so maybe they thought I might just have the answer. I took a moment to look around the room before I began speaking. Arnë had been right. These people were seriously ill. Everyone of them had a ghostly grey pallor and they appeared listless and unhappy. They were also all women. I could feel a rising panic as I launched into what I had to say. A small pathetic voice in my head was saying, how can you help? You have only just started out in this. You don't even really know what you're doing! I shut it up and sallied on for about half an hour before I ran out of steam.

"Well, if anyone would like a session, I am going to be here for the rest of the day so just have a word at the desk and make an appointment," I finished.

I couldn't wait to get out of the room. I bumped into Arnë in the hall.

"How'd it go?" he grinned.

"Don't ask," I grunted heading towards the kitchen. I needed coffee.

Bizarrely, as I reached the door to the kitchen it swung open and a tiny wizen faced woman with a bad stoop emerged carrying a jug of dark brown liquid. I could smell the aroma. I was pretty tuned into the smell of coffee. It was definitely one of my perks in life.

"Ah, coffee for you too," I quipped as I held the door open for her. She looked too frail to manage it on her own.

She looked up at me slightly quizzically, then smiled.

"I prefer to drink it," she whispered hoarsely. Her voice sounded hollow and empty.

"Enema," Arnë whispered in my ear.

He had silently come up behind me. He had a habit of doing that. The woman didn't say anything else just made her way slowly up the wide flight of stairs to the second floor with all the effort of climbing Everest.

Well I took my coffee straight—straight down my throat that is! Afterwards I checked at the desk and with surprise and delight saw that three people had booked a session with me. Hmm, must be my boyish charm. Women seemed drawn to it—especially older women and I had to admit that often the feeling was mutual. I definitely found older women a lot more interesting than those of my own age and always had done. I saw the first before lunch. I was extremely anxious but hey it was also a challenge. I wasn't really sure what I was to do but I keep the treatment regime simple and just tried to really connect. The hour session passed smoothly. As was usual after one of my sessions, my client left feeling calm and emotionally better. I breathed a sigh of relief and started to get excited about lunch.

My excitement was justified. The meal was great. Lots of imaginative salads, kidney beans, sweet corn and chickpeas in herb and garlic and olive oil dressing, couscous with fresh mint and lemon, raw beetroot and carrots with caraway seeds and a spicy vegetarian lasagne. Delicious! I gave the glasses of thick green wheatgrass juice a miss though. I overate, and as a consequence, had a hard time staying awake enough to get through the two sessions of the afternoon. By the end of the day I had decided that it wasn't so bad and that I would like to work there. I offered my services every Thursday.

After a few weeks of this regime things were beginning to unravel. The pressure of trying to run two separate businesses was beginning to take its toll. When I was in the bookshop I wanted to be at the Tree of Life Centre and when I was there I needed to be in the bookshop. I was also becoming increasingly in demand at the Park Centre and on some Thursdays I'd arrive to find that ten people had booked to see me! Whilst this was deeply gratifying it was also exhausting. Some evenings I would struggle not to fall asleep at the wheel of the car on the way home and have to pull over and sleep for a while before arriving home at nearly midnight.

There was also the Tai Chi class that I had started up again on my return from San Francisco. That took up another evening. The numbers in the class had now dwindled down to three. There was an older woman who was an ex yoga teacher. She had made the transition to Tai Chi pretty well. They don't all I had found. They were usually great on flexibility of body but their minds were rarely as pliable and their co-ordination was often weak. There was also a guy who had joined quite recently. He was a bit stiff but he showed promise and then there was Megan, she of the streaked hair and the wedding band. I had noticed that I actually looked forward to Tuesday evenings when I knew she would come to the class. She was friendly, sometimes amusing, always hard working and questioning. She stimulated me in more ways than I cared to admit. No I didn't want to give up the Tai Chi class!

Meanwhile my cloak of invincibility was definitely losing its shine. Gradually I noticed that my chest was beginning to play me up again. It started fairly innocuously. A few whistles and wheezes, a tight sensation, like a band around my chest, and an annoying headache. It came to a real head one Thursday as I struggled to breathe whilst giving my final session of the day to a delightful blue rinsed lady ravaged by the cancer in her bones. It was crazy. I was supposed to be healing her and yet I felt like I was the one that was dying.

The following Friday morning I ran into Arnë in the street.

"Arnë, I'm loosing it," I said. "You have to do something about this. I can't go on like this any longer."

Arnë looked at the pallor of my skin and the mist of sweat on my forehead, the tension in my raised shoulders and the pleading in my eyes.

"I have a session at the Tree of Life in ten minutes," he said. "I'll see you later at the bookshop."

When he came into the shop a couple of hours later he didn't speak until the place was empty. He had been passing the time until the last customer left by walking slowly up and down in front of the bookcases pretending to be interested in the selection, although he knew them all pretty much by heart by now. He had stopped and was fingering one of the china Tai Chi figures on the top shelf when he finally spoke.

"What you think about going into the collective unconscious?" he asked.

"What do you mean?" I answered. "You don't mean past lives and all that stuff do you? I don't believe in them."

"Well, I don't much care whether you do or not," he said. "I was just asking what you thought about it."

There was a pause, then he continued in a some what matter of fact voice. "I think there is something much deeper going on with your chest and I think we can get to the bottom of it. Are you willing to at least give it a try?"

Hell, by now I'd have stood on my head and whistled Dixie if someone had told me that it would help!

"Okay, okay," I replied. "When?"

"Saturday."

PRESENT FROM THE PAST

Arnë and I decided to work in his room at my Centre. It was a smaller room at the back of the house on the first floor. Its window overlooked the patio area and garden but it never really got direct sun. Nevertheless it was a nice room. It still had the old black cast iron Victorian fire place and two really comfortable arm chairs plus a small coffee table. There was nothing else in the room. Even the walls were bare. Arnë liked it that way.

I sat down in one of the chairs and Arnë moved the other so that it was opposite me. He took off his jacket and sat down.

"Right Hugh. Just sit back in the chair and relax. Close your eyes and just watch your breath."

I was immediately transported back to the last time that we had worked on my breathing problem together back in my small apartment. I let my mind drift along with what he was saying as he gradually got me more and more relaxed.

I heard him say.

"You are drifting along in a small boat. It is warm and sunny and you lie back in the boat as it drifts slowly along and begin to relax in the warmth of the sun. You can feel the warmth of the sun spreading, spreading slowly throughout your entire body... and as you feel the warmth spreading you allow yourself to relax even more, relax into a deep... deep sleep. That's right. Drifting off into sleep now. Drifting on getting sleepier and sleepier. Ahead of you lush green ferns grow at the mouth of a large cave, and slowly... slowly the boat begins to drift towards it. The yawning mouth of the cave is wide and inviting. It

looks cool and refreshing in contrast to the sun's heat. As you drift along, drifting deeper and deeper asleep you feel the pull of the cave and you want to go in. Slowly, slowly you feel yourself pulled into the cave. You feel safe and supported in your boat, just drifting... drifting. Deeper and deeper you go, deeper and deeper still... into the cave."

My attention seemed to be pinpointed on the sound of Arnë's voice. I was aware only of the sound of his voice and a warm, velvety sinking feeling. In the distance I heard Arnë instructing me to go back in time. I continued to drift. It was warm and dark and I continued to drift. Suddenly I was in my mother's womb. I had to get out! I had to escape! I could feel a rising sense of panic. I was being poisoned and if I was to survive then I had to get out and quickly. Later I found out that my mother had toxaemia when she was carrying me and it was indeed a toxic environment for me to be in.

Whatever this revelation was Arnë, obviously decided that it was a possible cause, but not the only cause of my present breathing problem and instructed me to go back further. I was unaware of it at the time but he was also keen to move me out of my present state of agitation and back to a sense of calm. This time I became aware of being someone else. My body felt small and tight. Lifting my hand I stroked down the side of my cheek, over the smooth hair there and tugged gently at the neat beard at my chin. There was a bustle of people around me and the air was dry and dusty.

"Where are you?" Arnë asked.

"The Middle East somewhere." I answered in a slow drawl. It was difficult to speak. My brain and my voice didn't connect. I felt that I was this young man. I looked out through his eyes, felt through his body, answered with his voice, yet there was also a part of me that was distant from him, watching, paying witness to what was transpiring.

"What are you?" came the next question. "What are you

34

doing?"

"I'm a Christian missionary priest."

A few more questions followed.

This life still did not seem to satisfy Arnë. He encouraged me to go back even further. My mind let go of the images around me and the young man began to fade. There was black. A great nothingness and time seemed to go on and on and still nothing happened. I could still hear Arnë encouraging me to go back. Go back and find a life that was relevant and important to this present one.

Then it happened. I became aware of my body changing suddenly—of looking out over an immense expanse of sea—a warm breeze blowing the hair away from my face—and an immense feeling of physical and spiritual power.

"Who are you?" came the sound of his distant voice.

"I am not sure," I heard myself saying. There was a long pause.

"I am a priest."

"Where are you a priest?" Arnë's voice came to me from along way off.

Again a long pause.

"I am a priest magician."

These last words, unlike those that had proceeded them, I spoke with power and authority. As the words left my lips I was suddenly projected out of the chair, at least it felt like I had been projected out the chair, for I suddenly seemed to be on the other side of the room looking at myself in the chair. As I looked at myself, the face of the 'me' in the chair seemed to be changing. It was growing darker and changing form. My body was also flailing about in the chair like I was having some kind of seizure! This was seriously weird! Whilst I seemed to be aware of everything that was taking place my mind was telling me that I could not be in two places at once and if that was a fact, then who the hell was that sitting in the chair? Come to that who was that by the wall? Hell! Which one was me?

It was Arnë's turn to go quiet. Then he spoke again only this time he did not speak in English. He spoke in a strange language that sounded like a bad case of the hiccups. It was jerky, full of vowels sounds.

"Aloha kāua, ʻO wai kou inoa?

Then out of my mouth, the one on the chair that is, I heard myself answer in the same strange tongue.

E noa! E noa! ʻĀmama, ua noa, lele wale aku la!

For sometime the conversation flowed back and forth between us in this strange tongue. Arnë then slowly began bringing me back from the deep place that I had got into. I was suddenly back in my body again and things calmed down somewhat. Arnë continued to question me but now I answered in English. I say, 'I', although it wasn't really me that was talking. At least it was me, in that it was my voice, but as Arnë posed each question a strong voice in my head answered and I felt compelled to voice what was said. When asked where I was, I answered;

"In Kaua'i."

Then the voice started to give information that Arnë had not particularly asked for. I was to prepare myself for weird and surprisingly strange happenings. I was also to start increasing my food intake over the next six weeks in preparation for the enormous changes my nervous system and my body were about to undergo. Then there was silence.

It was at this point that Arnë obviously decided enough

36

was enough. He started bringing me out of the altered state that I was in. Then one of those strange things that the voice had warned me about happened. Almost immediately I was propelled out the chair and across the room, only this time it was for real. I could see the wall coming at me. There was no way I was going to stop and I slammed into it. Turning round I slid down the wall and sat laughing hysterically like a hyena. I couldn't stop. I don't know how long I sat there laughing like a loon until I finally came to my senses but when I eventually did I felt exhausted. I looked across at Arnë. He was grinning. I noticed that he was soaked in sweat.

"You don't know whether to laugh or cry do you," he said.

"What the hell was that about?" I shouted.

"God knows," said Arnë.

I was not reassured.

"But," Arnë continued, "the last time I saw someone's aura change like that I was with the Xingu tribe in Brazil."

"What in God's name were you doing there?" I said. My mind was beginning to spin again and I felt suddenly nauseous.

"Years ago I took time out and went to study the healing practices of a few shamans around the world," Arnë said in a very matter of fact voice.

"As you do!" I thought.

He continued as if delivering a travelogue.

"I've lived and worked with the Taulipang in Guyana and the Ayahuasquero in the Amazon among others."

"So what was all that about?" I repeated.

"Well, I guess it was our Hawaiian past catching up with

37

us," Arnë said, still grinning.

That was it! I couldn't sit there any longer, besides my insides were churning like a can of worms. I made a dash for the door. I almost didn't make the bathroom! When I emerged, considerably relieved and slightly refreshed from a hurried splash of water to my face and neck some minutes later, I found Arnë downstairs in the kitchen. He was standing looking out of the window as motionless as a statue. He had a unique way of standing. I had noticed it in the shop when I had first met him and he was exhibiting it now. He would stand with his heels together and his toes pointing outward at about sixty degrees. His knees were always locked back and his back ramrod straight. The overall effect, given his slightly portly figure, was one of a king penguin. So here he was a penguin who had travelled around the world, observing no doubt all sorts of weird shit in the process, standing stock still and bemused in my kitchen. I was beginning to realize that I really knew next to nothing about this man. I wasn't sure what I wanted to say to him. As it was it was he who spoke first.

"I'm not sure I can give you a full explanation for what has just taken place," he said slowly and gravely, "but I can tell you that I too have a full recollection of a strong Polynesian connection and now, it seems, so do you. What this has to do with your chest I don't know at the moment but I can tell you that it is highly significant to your life at the moment."

"In what way?" I asked.

"Can't say," Arnë replied. It seemed to me that there was a lot that he didn't know or maybe it was just that he wasn't telling me.

"Oh God," I thought, "now I'm getting paranoid on top of everything."

There was a period of silence. Arnë stood looking out the

kitchen window and I stood staring dumbly at his back.

"Let's get a coffee," he suddenly said.

I could only hope that things would get clearer as time went on because right now I was feeling completely in the dark. Arnë got his jacket. I noticed that his shirt was still quite damp. He must be feeling uncomfortable, I thought, but it seemed inappropriate to offer him one of my shirts so I let him get on with putting his jacket on.

Once outside I realized how very peculiar I was feeling. The contrast from the world I had just emerged from and the bustle of the town street was mind blowing. The noise assaulted my ears until they hurt and in the time we had been inside the Centre someone had painted the town in bright luminous colours. My eyes seemed to have to widen to take everything in. I also felt enormous. Of course I wasn't any different in size to what I had always been but my sense of myself was that I was taller and bigger all around. I also felt tremendously energized. My body was fizzing and tingling all over. As we made our way to the coffee bar people seemed to be moving out of our way as if we had some kind of contagious disease. One young boy even stepped off the pavement into the path of an oncoming car. The blast from its horn cut through me like a knife. I felt I had no defences, that in some way I was wide open so that everything and everybody was impacting on me and I seemed to be having a similar effect on the people around me. "Bizarre!" I thought to myself. I also had this strange thought in my head that everyone that came near me, as I walked up the road, was being somehow irretrievably changed by just walking through my energy field.

"I've got my invincibility back and how!" I chuckled half under my breath.

"What did you say?" Arnë asked.

39

"Oh nothing. How are you feeling?" I responded, suddenly wondering if he too felt the change that had occurred around us.

"Well," he said slowly. "When I finished the session, I felt as if I was God! Now, the overwhelming need for cappuccino has brought me back to earth and I realise that I am just Arnë again."

Suddenly and inexplicably we both started laughing. What a ridiculous pair we must be, I thought to myself, a loon and a penguin walking up the street. Strange birds indeed!

The feeling of omnipotence continued and on the night of the Tai Chi class I was still feeling pretty manic. I felt like I was high on some cosmic juice. I had always been a great talker but on this night I just didn't stop. The practice room at the end of an hour was as charged as I was. There was only Megan and Sue, the ex-yoga teacher, in the class that night. I decided we would finish off with a standing meditation. The two women positioned their bodies in the posture 'Stork Spreads Wings' and stood motionless. The atmosphere was intense and I could see Megan's body swaying slightly as she continued to hold the posture. I walked over to her and lightly placed my hands on her shoulders intending to steady her, instead she dropped like stone and lay sweating on the floor at my feet. Sue was alarmed. Me too! I dropped to my knees and looked hard at her, staring intently into her dark grey eyes.

"Are you Okay?" I asked. You know the dumb question you always ask when someone clearly isn't!

"I thought I was going to black out," she said. "I'll be okay in a minute."

I decided that I would finish off the class with a short meditation. That way Megan could stay lying on the floor without risk of harm. I took them through a short relaxing meditation and then sat quietly in the semi darkness as the

40

two women lay stretched out with their eyes still closed. Then I got to my feet and crouched down beside Megan intending to check in with her. Instead I said, and I don't know why I said it but I did

"What would it mean to have someone say to you over and over again, *I love you?*"

That was enough for Sue. She freaked.

"I'm going," she said, and scuttled headlong out the door.

Megan stared back at me and gave me a broad smile.

"You rat," she said.

It was, I thought, a strange response. It was as if she had been playing some kind of game and I had found out, or she had been hiding and I had somehow found her. It wasn't making a lot of sense but I was pleased to see that the colour was back into her cheeks by now and she sat up.

"I think I should go now," she said.

"Sure," I said, yet I felt compelled to repeat, "but I meant it, what would it mean if someone told you again and again, *I love you?*"

She suddenly looked incredibly sad and I wished that I hadn't pushed the point.

"I'm going," she said. "See you next week."

Things were, I decided, becoming decidedly weird around here, but if I thought that was weird then what transpired later was way off the scale.

The first time it happened I was driving to the Park Centre. I knew the road really well by now and so I suppose I was driving pretty much on autopilot. As my mind started to drift my vision became just ever so slightly blurred. I could still see the road but what was more present in my field of vision was a dark face. I braked instinctively and the car slowed. The face remained in front of me.

"What the..."

As I tried to stare more intently to discern the detail of the face it disappeared. Then the voices started, or to be more specific, *the* voice. It was talking in the same strange tongue that Arnë and I had been using on the day of the 'collective unconscious' experience. I pulled into the next lay by and stopped the car. I rubbed my face vigorously with the palms of my hands as if trying to rub out the experience. It worked. There was no face and no voice. Feeling relieved I continued on with my journey. The experience haunted me though and I found myself dwelling on it as gave the day's sessions.

CONFUSION

'THE ART OF TRYING TO UNDERSTAND THAT WHICH YOU DON'T KNOW, BY
THAT WHICH YOU DO'

Back home after the Tai Chi class, Megan was also desperately trying to make sense of what was happening to her. Jack was already asleep in bed when she got in. She hadn't hurried straight home after the class, feeling the need to steady herself first by driving around. She was troubled and this was not the first time that she had found herself so bothered. Hugh had had the strangest effect on her right from the first moment that she had walked into his class. There had been more students then and at the beginning there was the usual round of introductions and reasons for attending the class. Megan had deliberately waited until last before announcing her name and the fact that she had seen a Tai Chi demonstration on television some two years previously. Although she had missed the beginning of the programme and didn't even know what it was called, or even the purpose of such exercise, she had known instantly that she wanted to learn it. Hugh had nodded attentively as she spoke as he had done with all the others.

"Well," he had said, "I'm not going to make a big effort to remember all your names because I know that most of you won't continue with the class for long. People never do. It's not what it seems."

Megan had felt her hackles rising. You'll remember my name, she thought to herself. At the time she had put her response down to her trait of always rising to a challenge. She had been like this all her life. As soon as somebody said you can't do this or you can't do that she had no resistance, she always took the bait. What happened later in the class had made her doubt that her reason for saying such a thing at this time was just her conditioned response.

Hugh had started the class with a few warm up exercises and then towards the end of the class said that he would teach the first few moves of the form so that we had something to work on before the next class and would hopefully start to get a feel for the system. He had demonstrated the first move and the class copied. Megan moved her body into the first posture. It felt good. She wasn't sure why it felt so good, after all it was only one movement. However, the slowness of the movement and the intent had a strong effect on her.

"I'm going to like this," she thought.

Then Hugh had got everyone to stop and hold the posture so that he could come around and correct it. He gave a few tips and hints to each person and repositioned their body so that they had a 'felt sense' of how the posture should be. Megan had waited patiently as he made his way through the group. She felt that she had got it pretty well. Hugh stood in front of her for a moment studying her stance, then took one arm and moved it, touching it lightly at the elbow to encourage it to relax and sink a little and at the shoulder to ease the tension from it. The moment his hands settled on her body, Megan felt her whole body respond to his touch. It softened and seemed to melt a little, then her entire body reached out to respond to the contact. It felt like coming home. It felt as if her body recognized something in him and was responding to the call. She had never experienced anything like it before. She was afraid that if he left his hands on her any longer she would melt and maybe even lose consciousness. Fortunately he moved on.

As she had continued to attend the classes the effect of his touch on her body continued. In fact her body grew to need it. A mile or so from the class as she was driving in each week her body would start to tremble in anticipation of the contact.

As she entered the class she felt sure that it was obvious to everyone and she fought to control it. It was like a drug, as soon as she started the class and he came around to reposition or correct her, her body got its' fix and felt content again. More and more it had seemed the contact between them had increased. She wondered if it was just driven by her need or if maybe he too was getting something from the contact.

Their relationship had certainly changed too, of course, as time had gone on. A friendly banter had started to emerge during the class sessions. It was easy and relaxed. She began to wonder if it was the Tai Chi that had her hooked or him. She was also concerned, married women weren't supposed to feel drawn in such an intimate way to another man. She convinced herself that this was different. It wasn't the usual sexual attraction that she, like most married people, flirted with in harmless ways over the years. Hmm, who was she kidding? She was sexually attracted to Hugh but she could deal with that. It was this other thing, this deep, old connection that she was unnerved by. There was a lot about him that she didn't even particularly like. His arrogance for one thing or maybe that was just a bit too close to home for her. It was a trait that she had often been accused of.

You'll remember my name, what had that been about? She tried to push all these thoughts out of mind as she crept into bed beside Jack. In some ways she resented him being there. He worked away a lot and she had the double bed to herself much of the time. She enjoyed stretching out and hogging the entire mattress. When Jack was home she had to contain herself, lie still and most of all crowd out her thoughts lest he should hear them and find her out.

She lay still as a corpse on her back staring at the blue outline of the window where the curtains didn't quite blot out the moonlight. She contrasted the feeling of containment she felt now with the aliveness in her body when she left the classes and a deep sadness infused her being. Then there was what had happened this evening. What was that all about? What was it Hugh had said?

"What would it mean to have someone say to you over and over again, *I love you*?"

What had he meant by that!? Was he saying that he loved her? She felt her heart race as she allowed that thought to surface. Or did he mean hypothetically, what would it mean if someone said that? She felt the question addressed some core issue deep inside her. Had she ever really felt loved and what would it mean if she ever did? She realized that by asking the second part of the question she had already answered the first part. God she couldn't be thinking about this now—not with Jack lying beside her. Jack said he loved her of course and that being the case how come she didn't feel it? How come it didn't impact on her? How come she couldn't respond to him the way that she reacted to Hugh?

I've got to stop this, she thought to herself as she shot a glance at Jack's motionless back beside her. She didn't know if he was awake or asleep. There was no response to her climbing into bed with him, but then with Jack there was rarely any response to anything anymore.

The next morning she fixed breakfast and packed Jack and the kids off to school. Some mornings it was her turn to make the school run. She would pick up the other kids on the way, set them off at the gates and then go shopping or return home to work in the garden. She could never settle to much on the days that it was her responsibility to get everyone to and from school. The journey back and forth took nearly an hour and doing it twice a day really ate into the day but today—today it was Jack's turn and she waved them off, thankful for the whole day to herself. She was still puzzling over the events of the previous evening. What exactly had he meant she kept asking herself and received no reply. She washed the dishes

46

then took a cup of tea into the lounge and slumped in the chair, staring vacantly out of the window, watching the long branches of the willow waving gently in a slight breeze. When the phone rang she was startled. The tea, now long cooled, slopped in the cup and she held it away from her so as not to get it down her shirt.

"01423 77982," she said, in what her kids called her telephone voice.

"Hi," said the deep warm voice at the other end.

It was Hugh. Megan recognized the voice immediately even from just this one syllable. She felt slightly panicked and yet underneath the panic there was the undisguised pleasure of hearing his voice.

"Oh, hi," she said brightly, trying to sound light and cheerful. "How are you?"

"I'm okay," he said. "I'm phoning to see how you are. You gave me a bit of a fright last night, are you feeling alright this morning?"

"Oh yes, sure. Right as rain!" Megan gushed.

There was an awkward silence. Then an eternity later Hugh said that he was pleased she was okay and they said their goodbyes.

When she put the phone down, Megan felt slightly dizzy again. She returned to the lounge and sat down. She felt thrilled that he had taken the trouble to inquire after her and she luxuriated in the recall of his velvet voice and the warm connected feeling it gave her yet she also recognized a slight chill of fear. She could feel herself shaking slightly. Where is this going she asked herself.

The next Tai Chi class could not come soon enough for Megan. She practiced the bits of the form every morning as

47

soon as she was alone. The slow connected flowing movements calmed her. They became addictive, a morning ritual that was all her own. Something she did for herself because it made her feel good. Like most mums she was used to life being played around the main players of husband, children, and home. Her bit part, essential as she knew it was, left her feeling undernourished and with a deep yearning for centre stage. She wanted to be noticed, wanted to be appreciated, acknowledged, wanted the starring role once in a while. Was that too much to ask? Maybe that was what the thing with Hugh was all about she mused. Maybe she just enjoyed the attention she got for that hour and a half a week, enjoyed the way it made her feel, like she was real person. She was confused. It was that of course, but there was something more, something that she couldn't get a handle on. Something locked away inside her that she had glimpses and memories of but had lost the key to unlock. Somehow when she was with Hugh those tantalising glimpses became momentarily clearer. When at the end of the next class he had asked her if she wanted a short healing session because he had learnt this new system called Polarity Therapy and he wanted people to practice on, she had leapt at the opportunity. It wasn't so much that she felt that she needed healing but that she knew it meant having Hugh's hands on her body. She had begun to realize how touch starved she felt. Jack had never been one for cuddles and hugs whilst she was very tactile by nature.

"Get off, leave me alone," Jack would say laughingly whenever she tried to move in on him to snuggle into his body and share the contact. The laugh made it sound casual but the message was clear.

She moved in on him less and less these days. She didn't know how she had coped with the rebuttal all these years.

"What's the matter," she would say, "is there something

48

wrong?"

She knew of course that there most certainly was. In fact, probably more than one thing. Jack seemed to have difficulties with just about everyone around him. He found it hard to open up and express himself to anyone. She could feel from his tight body how he locked down the everyday hurts and experiences that he found hard to deal with. She longed for him to just talk to her about them, share them with her, but he just kept pushing her away, dealing with it all the only way he knew how, with silence, cigarettes and alcohol. No wonder she felt lonely so much of the time!

Hugh turned down the lights in the Tai Chi studio and Megan lay out on the floor. At least if she felt faint again she would already be horizontal she thought as he took her head in his hands. His hands were large and extremely warm. Megan felt the muscles in the back of her neck starting to relax and let go in to the safety of his touch. A spontaneous deep breath lifted her chest and she felt her body unravel more as she let the air escape slowly through her nose. She didn't know how long he sat just holding her head. She floated on a sea of eternity. She was no longer aware of her body at all. She could feel strong pulsations of energy moving through her, flooding from the contact on her head down to her feet in rhythmic waves. It was the most peaceful, pleasurable sensation she had ever experienced. She heard, rather than felt, Hugh move around to the side of her body. He placed one hot hand on her chest and the other on her abdomen and began rocking her. Once again her body responded to the contact, moving away gently in response to his push and then returning again, naturally seeking his touch so that it might be moved again. It was a rhythmic pulse of life, a tide of energy between them, she the passive beach, he the water reaching out and then receding leaving the sand pregnant with the flood, yet eagerly awaiting the next wave, insatiable. Then the movement stopped. Her body fizzed and tingled as the energy spread through it, then there was calm. She felt herself expanding, getting lighter and then, impossibly, magically, his warm hand slipped effortlessly inside her chest. A tiny part of her conscious mind kept saying that it could not be so and yet she had the very real sensation that his hands were very definitely inside her. The merging was complete, the feeling ecstatic!

After what seemed a long time, Megan returned from a far away place. Hugh was sat crossed legged beside her just watching. She turned her head toward him. There was strange light in the room. They seemed to be enveloped in a cloud of blue and the air seemed thick and intense.

"How was that," he said.

"Incredible!" Megan responded. "God, I felt that your hands went right inside me and now—well now I feel great, calm and warm and safe and I don't know, real somehow."

There didn't seem to really be the words to describe what she was feeling.

"Thanks," she said. "Thanks a lot, that was great."

"You're welcome," he replied and stood to turn up the lights. "See you next week. Keep practicing."

Megan gathered her thoughts along with her jacket and moved to the door.

"Thanks again," she said. "Bye."

Hugh watched her go, aware of the abrupt way in which he had terminated the session, but he was feeling frazzled. He couldn't believe the connection that he had just felt with this woman. He was used to energy sensations and body shifts by now in the sessions that he gave, but there had been a deep and peaceful and total merging with this woman that was unique. He too was puzzled and not a little confused. He felt he really knew this woman, had known her all his life. Maybe it was recognition. Had he known her before? The connection was just so easy and so strong. Driving home, Megan was wondering the self same thing!

THE WEIRD AND THE WONDERFUL

Well it was true. My life was becoming more and more weird by the day. The dark face that had first become apparent on my drives to the Park Centre now regularly floated into my field of vision on and off throughout the day. Even more disconcerting than that was the fact that I seemed to regularly bi-locate. I would be driving or washing up or doing a session and suddenly I would find myself on a beach looking out on an expanse of ocean, watching the spray spewing off the curl of the huge surf in front of me. It was sometimes an effort to drag myself back to ordinary reality, whatever that was. Nothing in my life seemed ordinary anymore! I was also having a peculiar effect on things around me.

Street lights would mysteriously turn on and off as I walked by, radiators banged and rattled in the room I was in and people were becoming more and more disturbed and upset in my presence. Even old friends were giving me a wide berth and a couple of the therapists at the Centre quit because of the 'strange energy' there. Even Marge wasn't popping into the shop so regularly on any excuse. This really was serious. I was beginning to feel more and more isolated and having serious doubts about my sanity.

Each morning I would wake from a fitful night's sleep spent in chaotic dreams that I found hard to recall, but which left me feeling drained and uneasy. An old friend was staying with me for a while and after one particularly traumatic night which, for a change, I did recall in the morning where I had seemed to be battling with a black magician, he came down to breakfast and announced he was leaving.

"I don't know what the hell was going on last night but I got no sleep at all and I can't stay here any longer."

I had no explanation for him and certainly no reassurance I could offer. Night time certainly did seem to be the time when lots of strange phenomena occurred and I remembered last night as being particularly distressing. The Centre was situated on a ley line, this I knew. What I wasn't aware of until later was that there was a witch of dubious repute who had a cottage some five miles away on the same ley line. Last night had been, it seemed, some kind of psychic battle with her. I decided that the strain of running the shop and the centre were not helping my mental state and so I came to the decision to let the shop go. The healing work I was doing was providing me with a lot more satisfaction anyway and I was getting some good results. People really seemed to appreciate what I was doing for them and even the patients at the Park Centre, sick as they were, got great benefit.

I pulled myself out of bed a few days later feeling leaden as usual after another frantic night. De-energised as I always felt after the night my energy would soon pick up through the day and was growing stronger, I could tell. A bright clear Spring sun streamed in through the bedroom window, illuminating a section of carpet and the pile of clothes that I had dumped on the floor the previous night. I had a day of sessions at the Centre ahead of me so shaking off the weariness of the night I walked naked into the bathroom. Rubbing my hand over the stubble on my chin I rested for a moment in front of the sink. I suddenly felt a little dizzy and reached out both hands to grab the sink to steady myself. My head bowed. The dizziness passed and I slowly lifted my head to gaze into the mirror in front of me. A pair of black eyes in a dark skinned face stared back at me. For once I actually managed to keep a relaxed gaze and the face, instead of disappearing instantly as usual, held steady in front of me. I noticed the long black hair, the broad forehead and slightly widened nose. Then I noticed a mark of some kind above the ridge of the nose on the forehead. I focused harder to get a closer look at what it was and the face faded so that I was once again face to face with my own familiar features.

That was the clearest picture yet of the person who had possessed me in that fateful session with Arnë. That was what it felt like, a possession. I no longer knew who the real me was and evidently nor did the people around me. Was I going mad? Oh God, what if I was really going insane? What if this was an immense psychotic break from which I might never recover? I could feel the panic rising in me again and my head buzzed dramatically.

The phone rang. It never ceased to amaze me how people would have the gall to ring at the most inappropriate hours of the day to change or make appointments. I always intended to leave the answer phone on out of office hours but invariably forgot and then felt compelled to pick up. As I replaced the receiver after the call I searched my brain for someone to speak to. Someone who was sane, someone who could give me an unbiased opinion of my mental state, but who? Certainly none of my old girlfriends would be any good. They could be pretty unstable themselves and they would most certainly have an axe to grind so any feedback I might get would certainly not be clear. Then I had it. I reached out to dial Megan's number. I wanted to speak to her. I wanted to seek her reassurance that I was okay that I wasn't going mad. I wanted to hear the calmness in her voice and imagine her smile at the other end of the line. She was real and we had no messy past history together and we had a good strong connection at some level. Reality prevailed however; as usual I was ravenous and if I was to get breakfast before my first appointment I had better go eat now.

My first client was a fifteen year old boy who was a county runner destined, it was said, for a great career in athletics. It was the only thing that the youngster lived for. He was passionate about running and pushed his body to the limits in the pursuit of faster and faster times. His reason for visiting me was a knee injury sustained several months ago that was proving resistant to treatment. He had already had physiotherapy on it and been to one of the best sports clinics before his brother, who was one of my old Tai Chi students, suggested he come and see me. I had given him half a dozen sessions already trying a myriad of Polarity techniques to relieve the pain. He came in, wincing as he climbed the fight of stairs to my treatment room. He lay down on the bodywork table and I gingerly placed my hand over his knee, half knowing what I would find as I did so. The knee was cold in relation to the rest of the leg. As I tuned into the energy in the leg it felt slow and sluggish, unresponsive even.

"It's no better is it Simon?" I stated flatly.

"No, not really," said the young man. "I have to make a decision tomorrow about the trials in eight weeks. I guess I'll have to pull out."

I registered the mixture of anger and disappointment in his voice.

"Well let's see what we can achieve today," I responded with false optimism.

I sat at Simon's head and tuned into the sensations in my hands as I held his head and waited for his body to relax and the breathing to deepen. In a short while the energy fields opened up and his breathing was steady. Moving around his body, I worked various parts to try to unlock the energy in his system and get it balanced and harmonised in order to optimise the healing potential. Finally I brought my stool around to Simon's side and, sitting down, took his knee in both my hands.

"What else can I do," I silently asked myself.

"That's easy," said the strong voice in my head.

I was becoming used to this kind of interruption by now so it came as less of a surprise as the days wore on.

"Okay," I silently answered, "if you are so clever tell me what to do."

"It's his spleen gateway," said the voice. "Put your left hand on the top of the knee and your right thumb on his spleen gateway and then wait."

"Spleen gateway?" I answered irritably. "I don't know where or what his spleen gateway is."

"Raise your right hand in the air, with your thumb pointing down," came the command.

I did as I was told. After all I had nothing to lose and Simon had his eyes shut so he had no idea what I was doing. I lifted my hand a two feet or so in the air. Almost immediately I felt a heavy weight on the back of my hand pushing it down onto Simon's body.

I closed my eyes and focused my full attention on Simon's knee. Suddenly, a large pounding disc of pain, about four centimetres across, materialised in the centre of my forehead. I thought I was going to pass out, it was that intense. At the same time Simons' knee began to get warmer. Despite the pain in my forehead I held the contacts. The warmth that had suddenly flooded into Simon's knee was increasing. In fact, it was increasing so rapidly that very soon, it was almost too hot to bear. I felt as if my hand was close to an electric fire. The heat was that constant and that intense.

Shit, I thought. If this gets any hotter I don't think I can hold on. I was feeling quite faint from the pain in my forehead. I could just see the headlines in the local rag: 'Strange Goings on at Healing Centre – Catatonic Therapist Found Slumped Over Client.'

However intense the discomfort I was determined to hang in there and see what would happen. Simon began snoring raucously. Gradually the pounding in my forehead slowed sufficiently so that I could move around the table and make the same contacts on the other side of his body. I then felt impelled to make strange little five pointed star patterns on each knee. Suddenly I felt my body wrenched away from Simon and I stood back, opening my eyes and breathing rapidly. I sat down Simon was still sleeping. I glanced up at the clock, wondering how much of the hour session was left. It was unreal. I thought that I had been working on Simon for some time but the clock revealed that in fact only twelve minutes had passed! I sat for a while, pondering what had just occurred. Finally, after another thirty five minutes or so, when I had fully recovered, I walked over to the bodywork table and placed my hand over Simon's chest and rocked it gently. He opened his eyes and turned to look at me.

"You're cured!" I stated.

"I find that hard to believe." said Simon.

"Me too," I replied. "But you're cured!"

I kept my next client waiting while I made myself a drink and tried to get my head around what had just occurred. It wasn't easy. I was still relatively new at the healing game and this was one manoeuvre that was definitely beyond me.

"Well, whoever you are, thanks," I finally said out loud as I placed the empty cup in the sink.

"That's just the beginning," said the voice again. "I have lots to teach you."

"Oh, God," I found myself saying aloud again. "I really am going nuts!"

Later that week, and indeed the following weeks at the Park Centre, my sessions became more and more powerful as

I received guidance and instruction from the now familiar voice in my head. I felt like a student receiving knowledge directly from a master. A lot of what I was told to do had no logic, or at least made no sense to my familiar frame of reference, but I quickly realized that the things that he told me to do had some powerful effects. Many of the people I saw at the Park were terminally ill so any cure would indeed have been a miracle. It was often impossible to follow up on their progress as they were only at the centre for a short time. The thing that I noticed time and time again was the sense of peace around the people I worked on. They would often be transformed by the end of the session and the room would fill with light and a sweet smell. One lady got off the table and, beaming from ear to ear, told me she didn't have to see me any more. That she felt fine. She died that night, peacefully.

I tried, as best I could, to keep things moving along in a normal fashion. But the strain was still immense. In the Tuesday evening Tai Chi class Megan arrived looking awful.

"I don't know what's the matter with me," she said. "I feel so bad."

"Come and have a session," I offered. "I'm free Sunday evening."

TASTE OF LOVE

"Come on up," I shouted from the top of the stair well as I heard Megan come in through the front door. I walked back into the treatment room and waited for her to arrive. I could see her turn to begin the climb up the last flight of stairs to where I stood. I was suddenly surprised and shocked. It seemed an immense effort for Megan to mount the stairs. She was making slow and uneven progress. Her normally bright face was ashen grey and her shoulders were rounded with fatigue. I was so shocked. She raised her eyes to look at me as she finally entered the room. They were dull and incredibly sad. I suddenly felt compelled to reach out and take her hands.

"Oh, my God Megan. You look awful!" I whispered. "Sit down."

I steered her towards the sofa and helped her to sit. I couldn't face her. I turned away from her and looked out of the window at the darkening sky. I heard myself take a long deep breath. I suddenly felt very scared.

"So what do you think is the problem?" I asked, still keeping my back to her.

"I don't rightly know," Megan responded, "but ever since I first met you I have felt that you are leading me somewhere and I can't help but feel that whatever is going on with me has something to do with you."

I could not disagree with her.

"I think you're right," I said, turning back to face her once more. "I've been going through some strange stuff lately.

Heavy duty, psychic events and I know that it been affecting the people close to me. Whatever you are feeling, I know it's my fault. I'm sorry."

Megan nodded slowly. She felt relieved. Knowing that what she was feeling had a real cause and that her suspicions had been correct seemed to lift some of the weight from her.

"Come on," I said, "lie on the table and let's give you a session."

Megan forced her ton weight of a body out of the sofa and over to the bodywork table. There was a calm in the room— that heavy peacefulness that is so common to places where lots of healing energy is present. A small table light spilled its glow in one corner of the room and the approaching night crept into the other corners, held at bay by the one small bulb. I took Megan's head in my broad hands and took a deep breath. Almost immediately I felt that connection that had been so strong the first time that I had treated her. Within three breaths we were breathing as one. As I waited there in the soft glow of the lamp, again the voice appeared in my head.

"Do as I instruct," it said. "I will tell you what to do."

Trancelike, I placed my hands in various positions on Megan's body, following the instructions that would help her to connect more intimately to her soul. I tuned in to the waves of sensation. I was beginning to trust this internal voice although I was still no closer to knowing who it was. Maybe it was me, just another part of my mind that I could suddenly access. Somehow I didn't think so. It sounded very distinct and yet a part of me at the same time. Maybe I really was schizophrenic. What ever the reason, the instructions I had been getting from the voice were always spot on. If the voice said do this and this will happen, it generally did so who was I to argue. In a short while I could no longer tell what was me

62

and what was Megan. We were one organism—a softly flowing amoeba in a sea of energy.

As soon as she felt Hugh's hands on her head, Megan relaxed and let go into the experience. She had no strength to resist and she had no inclination to do so either. She could not tell where his hands were on her body because she was overwhelmed by what was occurring inside her. The feeling of peace that she had experienced at the beginning of the session gave way to bliss. Never had she felt so wonderful, so full of love and at the same time so loved. Vivid colours expanded and pulsed in her head. Deep, deep purple and pink and dark maroon, then shades of green. Her body felt supported and warm. She felt open and completely trusting. Then, how long into the session she had no idea, there came a golden stream of energy that moved from the base of her spine, spiralling deliciously up through her neck and out of the top of her head, then, fountain like, the same golden stream cascaded down around and through her. It was ecstatic! Golden flecks of watery light surrounded and filled her.

"So this is love," a small voice in her head mused, "complete, unadulterated, pure love! Divine!"

It was the most amazing, the most complete, the most spiritual thing she had ever experienced. Everything, she suddenly knew, was perfect, just perfect. She didn't know how but she was convinced that God's love had touched her and that from this moment on she would never ever be the same again!

Like sleeping beauty, adrift in a thousand year sleep of unconsciousness, Hugh's kiss on her forehead awoke her to a new world where she could no longer fall into the sleep of habit and denial but where knowing and consciousness reigned. When she at last opened her eyes, the room was awash with a golden glow that dimmed the small table light,

63

and the air felt thick and heavy. She didn't register it but Hugh had moved from her head and was now standing by the fire place, one leg crossed over the other and one arm sprawled along the top of the mantle. It was one of his favourite stances. He had been standing in exactly that stance the first time that she saw him, she suddenly remembered, when she had turned up to the first Tai Chi class. He was staring at her. Megan sat up and, as best as she could, tried to find the words to explain the experience that she had just had. How could she put words to Divine Love. A love unlike anything that she had ever known or ever believed could be possible. A love stronger even than the love she felt for her family, her friends, anyone!

I stood watching her as she sat crossed legged on the bodywork table. I knew that something very unusual had occurred, something profound and quite scary in its immensity. She was surrounded in a warm glow. She was such a contrast to the grey dull figure that had staggered up the stairs earlier. I suddenly felt impelled to tell her that I had loved only a few people in my life and then it seemed the most natural thing in the world to tell her that she was one of them. As the words left my mouth I knew that I always had, not just for last few months but for always, been in love with her. I felt I had loved her a lifetime.

"I love you also," Megan replied.

She said it not as an automatic response, not out of need, nor pity but because it was true. True in its most profound sense. She might have felt a little like sleeping beauty but this was no romantic, idealised fairy tale that she was caught up in. She said it as a matter of fact. A truth that was plainly stated.

Rising from the table, she crossed the room and kissed me lightly on the cheek.

"Thank you," she said, and turned to leave.

I watched her go fighting the emotion that was struggling to burst forth from my chest. How can this be, I thought to myself, my eyes stinging as I fought back the tears. How can I have found this woman and she not be available? What's going on? It's just not fair!

I phoned her the next morning, and the next, and the next. I needed to talk with her, needed to find out if there really was a unique connection between us, needed her reassurance, her steadiness. She was in my mind every moment of the day and night.

BACK TRACKING!

Megan too felt him close to her all the time, so much so that she became confused as to what were her thoughts and feelings and which were his. They kept asking what each was feeling during their early morning calls, as if to establish ownership of all thoughts and emotions. To somehow prove that there was a distinction, a separation that both were keen to establish even though the reality was that it was becoming harder and harder to separate their being.

Megan was feeling more open and easier than she could remember feeling for a long time, if ever. It didn't take a genius to recognize that she was getting far more from this relationship with Hugh than she had ever got with Jack. For a start, she and Hugh could discuss anything. There was no topic that did not warrant their attention. Hugh also encouraged her to get into her feelings, something that she found extremely hard initially. Expressing her emotions was not something that had been encouraged in her life and Jack had very firmly put a brake on any thing remotely approaching getting in touch with deep feelings. We'll be okay, he would repeat like a mantra whenever things did not seem to be going well. As she spoke with Hugh, Megan came to realize that for much of her adult life she had actually felt quite isolated, depressed and hurt. Being practical and surviving were things that she had learnt to master through necessity. Suddenly, after all these years, just having Hugh listen to her validated her feelings and experiences and it all came as a great relief to her. Here, she felt was a true friend and confidant.

The Friday after the incredible session at Hugh's Centre, Jack and she had gone out for a drink. Going out for a drink was something that they used to do a lot at the weekends when she had been running her own business as well as looking after two small children and Jack was not working such long hours. They would eat supper at home, leave the children with the babysitter and walk the few hundred yards to the pub. Megan would have a few glasses of wine and Jack would usually get stuck into the beer, lots of it!

As they eased into a corner seat in the cramped pub that Friday evening, Megan looked hard at Jack. He looked tired. His job involved a lot more responsibility these days and she knew that there was a lot of internal politics running through the firm at the present which Jack was finding hard to deal with. He had also been dealt a few bad hands lately, losing commissions that were due to him and getting the knife in his back from one senior colleague in particular. She wished he would confide in her. Maybe he thought that she wouldn't be able to cope, or perhaps he was just too scared to open up to her. Perhaps he thought that she might not be able to deal with his weaknesses. Megan realized that she was sick of second guessing. Whatever the reason for the stalemate situation that they found them selves in at present it was probably the one that would persist as usual. After her second glass of wine Megan found the courage to speak.

"I'm concerned about us," she stated, looking over her glass to the far side of the room.

"What do you mean?" Jack responded defensively.

Megan took a deep breath, she had started now and she knew she had to go on.

"Just that," she said. "I'm concerned about us, about our relationship, and about our marriage."

Jack blanched and he put his beer down heavily on the

68

table.

"What do you mean?" he said weakly.

"Well, we never talk to each other, in fact we hardly even see each other these days. You are not happy, I'm not happy…" Her voice trailed off.

"What exactly are you trying to say?" Jack's voice rose in panic.

Megan suddenly lost courage. She wanted to talk with him, explain about Hugh, tell Jack that she still loved him but that she couldn't reach him, that that made her feel isolated and alone a lot of the time. She wanted to say all this and more but she could feel herself bottling out. Jack sounded so scared.

Megan paused. It was her turn to sound defensive. Slowly, she said;

"I'm just saying, things between us aren't as good as they could be. Maybe we could both make a bit more of an effort to appreciate each other and spend the time that we are together in a much more meaningful way. That's all!"

Jack just sat and stared at her. He looked like he didn't have a clue what she was talking about.

"You're not going to leave me?" he finally said. It was a question but it sounded more like an order.

"No, where would I go?" Megan responded. "I'm just saying let's make an effort for God's sake!"

The walk home had been silent. They looked in on the kids and undressed for bed without speaking. Jack was in bed first. Megan slipped in beside him. He was on his side facing the wall, his back towards her. She lay still as a board on her back beside him, staring up at the ceiling and sensing the hostility coming from him. Eventually she reached over and turned out the light. Jack didn't move.

Lying there in the dark, Megan came to a decision. She couldn't bear the thought of having to tell Jack that she was leaving. How would he react? Would he become violent? God, no, he wouldn't do that, and yet it would be an extreme circumstance, who knows how he would react? Then there were the children. How could she disrupt their lives, what would her friends say, what about the rest of her family, how would they take such a piece of news. It wasn't as if she was even having an affair! Hugh and she had done nothing but talk, share experiences. Alright she had had a couple of sessions from him and yes he still moved her body around in the classes but all that didn't add up to a physical relationship. Hell she'd had more physical skirmishes with some of Jack's friends in the days when they would all go out to functions together. She felt confused—no, not confused; she felt guilty. Guilty about what, she wasn't so sure, but that was what she felt never the less. Guilty and fearful. She couldn't go on like this. She had told Jack that they had to make an effort, that meant her as well as him so if she was to get this marriage back on track again she would have to give it her undivided attention. She would tell Hugh when he next phoned that they had to stop contacting each other. She also thought to herself, with not inconsiderable regret, that this would mean giving up the Tai Chi classes as well.

"But why," I asked when she told me her decision on Monday morning.

"Because I have to give Jack a chance," she replied. "I haven't been that hot to be around lately. I've been so preoccupied with you and maybe he has picked up on that. I'm not being fair. I have to focus on Jack and me for a while."

I couldn't believe my ears. I knew that I had been pushing the relationship. It was always me who initiated our morning calls, but I really valued having this woman in my life. I needed her. Okay, it was a clandestine relationship. Okay, if it wasn't right, she being a married woman, it wasn't exactly wrong either. I had come to really value and rely on the deep friendship that had grown between us and I had prided myself on not crossing the boundary between that friendship and a more intimate relationship. It wasn't that I didn't want it. It was just that it seemed inappropriate and Megan had made no moves in that direction and that was fine. The thought that I might not see her again was producing a feeling of acute desperation.

"Is this it then—forever?" I asked.

"I don't know. Please don't make it harder for me Hugh. We have to stop. I can't cope any longer."

There was an uneasy, powerful silence over the phone line.

"Don't forget me," I finally said. Not knowing what else to say.

"I won't." Megan responded. "I promise."

A discernable chill ran down my spine as I heard those words.

As she put down the receiver, Megan had an uncontrollable urge to vomit.

AN INTRODUCTION – WELL OVERDUE

 For the next few weeks I felt totally bereft. Simon had phoned me a couple of days after his session to say that he had decided to enter the National under 16's trials. He phoned again now to say that he had come third in his event and was well pleased given the time he had been out due to the knee trouble.

The only thing that provided a slight distraction from the nagging thoughts in my head about Megan was the information that I was receiving from the voice in my head. I had begun a sort of dialogue with it. Not content to just have it appear randomly, I wanted some interaction with it. Most of all I wanted some answers! It was becoming clear to me that the incident with Arnë had had far-reaching consequences that were only now beginning to make sense to me. The priest magician that I had 'become' on that trip into my deep sub-conscious was still with me I managed to ascertain from the voice that he was a Kahuna or priest that had lived on the Hawaiian island of Kaua'i about 600 A.D. Skilled in many healing and magical arts he seemed willing to pass on much of his understanding and experience to me, which at least explained the increase in efficacy of my treatments lately and some of the miraculous experiences such as the one that Megan had had during our session.

"But why me?" I asked one evening as I closed the door after the last client of the day.

"It had to be you," Kiri answered.

Yes, we were on first name terms by this time.

"I have been with you since you were born, just waiting for the right moment to establish a strong conscious connection with you," Kiri continued.

"And what defined the right moment," I asked.

"The moment when you would be open enough and emotionally challenged enough to let down your defences," he responded.

"You make it sound like some kind of psychic attack," I said.

Kiri laughed. It was good to know he had a sense of humour.

"Well yes, in a way it is. I'm certainly in your mind and as you may have noticed I have the ability to borrow your body for a while also. How do you think your sessions are getting that much better? I have an understanding of energy that is far beyond any of your current perceptions."

"So you are, what? Using my body for some purpose? I'm not sure I like the sound of that. You sound like some kind of parasite. What if I don't want to let you use it?" I asked.

Kiri laughed again. "Do you think you have a choice?" he said, and I had to admit to myself that there was no way I could stop him taking over or I would have done so by now.

"Don't worry, I won't do anything harmful with it. As to being a parasite, well, I like to think of it more as a symbiotic relationship. You have to agree that you are gaining a lot from this also," Kiri stated.

I already had a strong sense of that. I was able to manipulate the energy in someone's body much more effectively than I ever felt possible and I was able to read their minds to some extent. To know what was really bothering them and help sort it out. That experience of Divine Love that

Megan had tried to describe to me after her last session, was also occurring with some of the cancer patients I was working with. It gave them peace and relieved a lot of the fear that they were experiencing as their life force was ebbing away. It also gave them great clarity of mind. All of this was pretty remarkable but I still didn't have a clear sense of what Kiri was getting from our relationship. Maybe he was some kind of ghost that just missed having a body and wanted to borrow mine some of the time. Anyway as far as I knew I didn't have much of a choice in the matter so I might as well shut up and enjoy the benefits.

A little while after Megan's decision to terminate our friendship I heard that she had started to teach her own Tai Chi class in her home town. I was pleased. She had always been a good student and I felt sure that she would make an equally good teacher. She had been practicing religiously for about three years now and I was pleased that she hadn't just given it up along with me. The news also set up the longing again and I missed her more than ever. One day I decided to ask Kiri about her. After all, he seemed to have a lot of information, about a whole host of things, that wasn't readily accessible to me.

"I feel like I know her, really know her like an old friend," I said to him as I lay waiting for sleep one night.

Again the familiar laugh. "That's because you do," Kiri replied. "We all go back a long way."

"What do you mean? I don't understand any of this and don't give me all that crap about past lives either. I don't buy that!"

"You can be so difficult, so stubborn," Kiri said "Your scepticism is good but it prevents you from hearing the truth sometimes. Let me try and explain."

He wasn't always so willing to be forthcoming with

explanations so I awaited this one with bated breath.

"I came to you because your psyche is a match, a near perfect match to how I was when I lived in Kaua'i. I knew that through you I would be able to work out a little unfinished business that I have and I can't put right from where I am. So I attached myself to you, as it were, at your conception and waited. I've been watching over you all your life. I'm what is called a 'companion spirit'. I am closer to you than your own skin. A part of you and yet distinct at the same time. Sometimes I have sensed that you have been a little aware of me, but mostly you have been bumbling along with your life screwing up just like everyone else."

"Thanks a lot," I muttered out loud.

"You're welcome," he replied, seemingly unaware of the irony in my voice.

"Okay," I said rising to the bait, "so I understand that you need me to help you out with something but where does Megan fit in?"

"Megan. Well. Megan, too, has a companion spirit. A companion spirit which will enable me to complete that unfinished business of mine."

"Yeah, so what exactly is this unfinished business of yours?" I asked.

"That's no matter at the moment. It is important that I do not tell you as it may affect the outcome. Suffice to say that it is important that I, and the companion spirit of Megan, can come together once more," Kiri continued.

"So what you are saying is, Megan and I have some kind of enactment to do, something to work out together that is as a result of something that went on with you and this other companion spirit when you were alive. Hell, I'm assuming you're dead. You are aren't you?"

76

"Dead to your world maybe, but I am an immortal spirit. I only lack a physical body. That's why it's good to borrow yours from time to time," and he laughed again.

My mind was boggling. I needed time to think about all this. At one level it sounded like something out of science fiction; 'The Invasion of the Body Snatchers' or 'Night of the Living Dead.' On the other hand, it felt extremely real to me. I certainly couldn't ignore my new found abilities. Abilities I did not have before this Kahuna made his appearance in my life. Well appearance wasn't quite the right word. I hadn't actually seen him. Well, not all of him. I had of course got those glimpses of what I now knew was his face. God this was all so unreal!

Saturday mornings I usually stayed in bed late listening to the traffic noise building up outside. In summer it was remarkable, practically bumper to bumper all through the day, and woe betide you if you wanted to get from one end of the town to the other against the prevailing tide of holiday makers, or grockles, as the locals liked to call them. They wandered, snail like, along the pavements browsing the shops. Herds of holiday sheep in search for new pastures of souvenir trivia to take home. Today though I was feeling restless, so I got up and decided to face the masses and head for the wine bar for a cappuccino. The journey was slow as I knew it would be. People kept coming to an abrupt stop right in front of me as they glanced some trinket in a shop window or stopped to panic over some missing kid. I decided to be a bit more pro-active and started pushing my way through the crowd. I saw her before she registered me. I was taller than most of the herd so that put me at an advantage. Her hair was longer and she looked okay except that her face was set in a slight frown like she was worried about something.

"Hi Megan," I said when there was only one man and small child between us.

My voice seemed to snap her out of the trance she was in and she looked up in my direction.

"Oh, hi. How are you?' she said automatically.

"I'm alright," I said, "and you?"

"Fine," she said unconvincingly.

I had stopped to allow her to reach me and to continue our conversation. I had a lot to tell her, not the least about Kiri and the fact that she had something to do with all this. As she got level with me, a slight stumble, somewhere along the road, was gaining momentum into a shove as it passed through the crowd. Taking the shove in her back, she bumped against me, smiled, and after a momentary pause kept walking. I couldn't believe it. I had come so close to her again and now she was being carried away in a sea of heads. I turned to look after her. She didn't look back.

The coffee didn't do anything to improve my mood and the wine bar was busy. I was beginning to wish that I had just stayed in bed. I sat cradling my empty coffee cup in my hands and thinking about Megan. It had been great to see her, even for a moment. What I couldn't cope with was the fact that she had not stopped, not even for a few minutes. I wanted to know what was going on in her life—were things with her and Jack working out, how was her class going, and most of all, did she miss me? Most of all I wanted to know if she missed me! They were fruitless, self-indulgent questions that I knew I wouldn't get an answer to but I couldn't help posing all the same. I battled my way home and buried my head in a book, glad of its distraction.

The following Wednesday I had to see my solicitor. The sale of the book shop was going ahead and of course there was the necessary paperwork to sort out. I didn't feel too bad about letting the shop go. I had got the asking price for it and I was looking forward to just concentrating on everything else that was going on in my increasingly bizarre life. As I came out of Webster and Croft's offices I decided to pick up a few things in the supermarket and then drop off a book I had borrowed from the library. As I turned into Manor Road. I couldn't believe my eyes. Megan was walking towards me. I saw her hesitate a moment. She was obviously deciding whether to continue on her present trajectory or turn into the side street that was coming up on her left.

"Don't turn, don't turn," I caught myself saying under my breath.

She didn't. She walked straight towards me and this time a broad smile spread across her face.

"Hello, Hugh. We meet again. Unbelievable isn't it? I hardly ever come down this street," she said.

"Hi," I responded.

There were so many things that I wanted to say but at that moment I was just caught up with the smile on her face and the pleasure that it gave me. She was undeniably pleased to see me. I, too, was grinning wildly at her. For a while we seemed content to allow the contact to hold. It was delightfully familiar; neither one of us really wanted it to end it seemed.

"Megan," I finally found the courage to say, "I need to talk to you. Can we go somewhere and talk. Please?"

"Hugh, I can't." She suddenly looked sad. "I can't start this thing up again I'm only just getting used to not having you in my life. I'd better go."

She looked around as if scared that someone might catch us together and then crossed the road. Her step quickened as she hurried to the corner. This time she did look back fleetingly. The further away from me she went the more I felt a tightening in my chest. It was as if we were connected by some kind of rubber band that allowed us to pull apart but that tightened and strained the further away the contact became. All it wanted to do was snap us back together again.

"I hope it never breaks," I said aloud.

Megan was feeling the tug exert itself on her too. It was as if she had been punched in the solar plexus, leaving a gaping empty, black, tennis ball sized hole behind.

There was no way that I could leave things the way they were. I had to spend some time with Megan and explain all the crazy things that had been going on. She was the only person I felt would at least listen to what I had to say, even if she didn't totally believe it. Kiri kept impressing on me the importance of her knowing about him. He kept pestering me about it like a school boy asking his friend to ask a girl out on a date on his behalf. For myself, I couldn't get her out of my head no matter how hard I tried. My dual personality was now splitting into three. My head was constantly filled with Kiri's voice, my own questioning in return, and alongside all that, thoughts and feelings for Megan ran riot. I had to do something or I was in danger of going completely and utterly mad. I wasn't convinced that I wasn't already in that lunatic state and that all that was happening was some powerful figment of my imagination. In black despair one morning on my way to the Park Centre, I stopped the car and propelled myself into a phone box. Without hesitation I dialled her number. We hadn't spoken on the phone for weeks but as I waited for her to pick up the old familiar excitement in anticipation of her voice rippled through me. I felt I had to speak with her or explode.

"01423 77982."

"Megan, it's me," I gasped. "Please don't hang up!"

There was silence at the other end of the line. I waited for the click of the receiver being replaced. It didn't come.

"Are you still there?" I asked.

"Yes, I'm still here Hugh. I thought you weren't going to contact me. What do you want?"

She sounded angry. Not real mad but angry in an irritated way.

"Megan tell me I'm not going mad. I have this voice in my head all the time and my body is doing weird things."

"What sort of weird things?" she responded.

Well at least I had got her attention!

"Power surges. That's the best way I can describe them. They come when I'm working on people and then at other times too when I'm alone. I get really hot and my body seems twice it's natural size and I'm, I'm vibrating. My right arm seems to have developed a life of its own as well and it flails around uncontrollably when I'm trying to just sit and rest. Then there are the things that are happening around me too, like lights fusing and people are getting scared of having me around. I don't know what's real any more and I'm getting pretty scared."

There was pause at the other end of the line. Shit, I thought, I've scared her too. Now she'll never see me.

"Are you still working?" Megan asked.

She seemed to be changing the subject and I wasn't sure why.

"Yeah. I'm on my way to the Park now and I've been seeing clients at my Centre. As a matter of fact since all this started I've been getting pretty good results in the sessions I'm doing. Quite miraculous really."

"And you are eating okay and looking after yourself alright?" Her voice said calmly at the other end of the line.

81

"Well yes," I said. "In fact, I've become quite ravenous most of the time."

"Then I don't think you are going mad. If you are still functioning normally, whatever that is, in the real world, then I think you are okay. As to what is going on for you I haven't a clue."

I felt the relief flood through me. Her grounded common sense answer allayed a lot of my present fear. I was right to value her opinion. I knew she would understand. I knew she would listen and be sympathetic. Her positive response gave me the courage to continue.

"Megan," I said, "I have so many things that I need to talk with you about, please, please can't we meet up."

Again the silence.

"Okay, Hugh. Just one meeting. Please understand that it is not an excuse for us to get back to how we were. I am only agreeing to this because you sound so desperate and you are, or at least were, my friend."

"Monday morning," I interjected quickly. 'I'll pick you up at 9.30 a.m."

"All right."

I put the phone down and spun around to head back to my car. I had to end the conversation quickly before she changed her mind. Now all I had to do was decide where we should go and how I was going to explain all that had occurred in a meaningful way.

I needn't have worried. Kiri had very concrete ideas on that.

BATCOMBE

When Megan answered the door on Monday morning I was taken completely by surprise. She was wearing a long turquoise skirt and a matching blouse cut low at the neck. The colour set off her lightly tanned skin. She looked so feminine. That was a crazy thing to think at that moment but in the context of a martial arts class, or during a session or hearing her disembodied voice over the phone line I had never really thought of her in such a sensual, feminine way. She was just Megan. Now I found myself seeing her with new eyes and I really liked what I saw. For a moment I was lost for words as my eyes drank in the scene in front of me. As she turned to pick up her bag and keys from the hall table, the skirt swirled around her ankles. She closed the door behind her and made her way to my car. I still hadn't spoken. As I put the car in gear and pulled out into the stream of morning traffic I came out of my stunned silence.

"You look great," I said. "I've never seen you in a skirt before."

Megan just smiled and watched the road ahead. We sat in silence until I had left the main road and was making my way through the less dense traffic of the country road. I still had to concentrate. There may have been fewer cars around, but the winding, narrow roads were still a test of driving skill. I knew from past experience that people tended to take greater risks on these kinds of roads, often assuming that they were quiet and therefore safer, but visibility was generally much reduced as the hedgerows expanded through the summer months and the road twisted and curved out of sight. There were only rare places where two cars could pass comfortably. Country driving was as much an acquired skill as driving in the city. However the warm late summer's day was relaxing me and concentrating on the driving took my mind off what I had to say later. Megan too seemed more comfortable as the journey progressed.

I was heading for Batcombe woods, a magical place I had discovered several months ago. It was one of England's older and forgotten woods and the earth energy there was particularly intense. It seemed the perfect place to go where I knew that we would be undisturbed and I could tell my story. It also seemed to be important to Kiri that I took her somewhere secluded where we would be alone. About a mile out from the wood I began to recount some of the events of the recent months. I decided to leave the all the information about Kiri till last. The road ahead was bounded by an avenue of tall beech trees. Suddenly we began to snake around in a long drawn-out left hand bend. I remembered this bend particularly well. The energy suddenly shifted at this point and became very thick and intense. I knew there was an opening not far ahead that would allow us an access into the wood. I pulled into a small lay bay and stopped the engine.

"Ok we're here," I said opening the car door and stepping out.

"Oh, I didn't dream we would be coming to a wood," Megan said as she opened her door. "I really haven't come prepared."

She was looking down at the flimsy sandals she was wearing.

"Why didn't you tell me?"

"I couldn't," I replied. "Well that's not strictly true of course. I could have but I wanted this to be surprise. Isn't it great?"

Megan looked up a the canopy of trees above her head and nodded.

"Yes, yes it is. I'll be fine."

And with that we both set off into the wood, me leading with her a few feet behind. There was an unearthly quiet about the wood, broken only on occasions by the suddenly shrill of bird call. A deep carpet of rotting leaves softened our footsteps. The further into the wood we went the more it felt we were the only people in the world. Suddenly, I became aware of being watched—you know the feeling, it's pretty indescribable but absolutely real all the same. I stopped and Megan fell in behind me. Then I saw our watcher. A few feet to our right stood a doe, warm brown and dappled in the filtered sunlight. Her deep brown eyes focused intently on us. I turned my head to alert Megan to her presence but she had spotted her already. All three of us stood there motionless. We were transfixed, caught in the headlights of her eyes as she held us there in quiet spellbound wonder for I know not how long. I felt blessed. This naturally timid creature was standing just a couple of arm's lengths in front of us, bold and at perfect ease. It was a blessing on our visit and I telepathically told her as much. It was as if she had been waiting for such an acknowledgement for at that moment she turned and in a couple of effortless bounds was gone leaving a void in the forest and in me, too.

I continued walking. Megan was asking me lots of questions about my experiences of late. Lots of questions that I didn't have answers for but in searching for them I sometimes found clarity and sometimes Kiri's voice in my head provided the more elusive responses. Finally, Megan stopped in her tracks. Sensing this I turned round to face her. She was standing looking at her feet which were nestled in the ancient blanket of fallen beech leaves.

"If all that you say is true," she started, "if we accept that you are possessed, or something like that by this companion spirit called Kiri, who has something to do, but you don't know what, and he needs your body to do it, what has it all got to do with me? You said it was as much his idea as yours to get me here today, but what for?"

"I only know what little he has told me," I answered. "It seems that you also have a companion spirit and you are necessary for the completion of—well I don't know what exactly. Oh God, I feel awful!"

I suddenly felt nauseated and somehow out of it. The blood was pounding in my head something rotten and I was sweating profusely. As I stared at Megan's face it seemed to disappear. In fact the whole wood was disappearing. Suddenly everything went black.

Megan suddenly felt afraid. Hugh's body had gone rigid. His head had arched backward and his fists were clenched at his sides. She thought he was about to fit. But he didn't. He held the posture for about a minute whilst some kind of inner struggle seemed to be going on inside him. Then his head came up again and he looked down at her except that it wasn't his face hovering above her. Dark shadows changed the shape of his cheek bones which now looked much higher and well defined, his nose seemed wider and his eyes, instead of his usually hazel flecked green, appeared jet black. She also noticed that the set of his shoulders was different too. They seemed wider and more powerful. If all this wasn't enough to frighten the life out of her what came next certainly did! He spoke, but he spoke not in the warm rich tones that she had come to love about Hugh's voice but in a stilted, deep, rasping tone. The voice had an urgency about it that was frightening.

'Forgive me," he said his jet black eyes burning into her like live coals.

Megan had no idea what he meant or what she was supposed to forgive, but somehow she found the strength to stand her ground and look back into the dark face above her.

"You must forgive me," came the voice again, this time even more urgently, "please, please forgive me."

Megan still had no idea what she was being asked to forgive, but what was clearly palpable was the pain and the desolation in this man, and she could not help but acknowledge his heartfelt plea. Whether she understood or not she knew that what ever it was, whatever he had done that needed forgiving, she had no right to refuse. She felt his very life depended on it or the torment would crush him.

"I forgive you," she said, and then softer still, "I forgive you."

As the words left her mouth she was suddenly overwhelmed with love and compassion for this man. It was strong enough to cause her heart to beat frantically at the wall of her chest. She was compelled to reach out and embrace him. As she wrapped her arms around his chest and lay her head on his shoulder, a great sob escaped him. Then he was falling, his knees were buckling and Megan had to use all her strength and brace herself, digging her heels into the soft leaf carpet—sensing and finding a foothold. Hugh's body was big and heavy and it was lolling dangerously backwards towards a clump of bracken and thorn bushes. With one well timed heave she pulled him forward and he found his feet and his balance again. Stepping back but still holding on to his arms to steady him, Megan looked up into Hugh's familiar face once again. He was crying and she could feel him shaking violently. He sank to his knees and put his head in his hands.

"Oh, my God," he said, his breath coming in spurts. "I never want to go through that again. My God, the pain, the pain."

Megan sank to the ground, her turquoise skirt flooding around her like a small pool. She reached out and pulled the hands from his face.

"What was that all about Hugh, what was going on?" she asked insistently. She had had more than enough of all this and she wanted some answers!

"You died—well not you but your companion spirit—he came into me Megan. He said he wanted to give me some idea of why all this is so important to him. I could feel the pain, the anguish that he felt. It was unbearable. How can anyone live feeling like that?"

Hugh began crying again and Megan let him be for a while before badgering him with more questions.

"Why did he want me, or her who ever she is, to forgive him. Did he kill her?"

Hugh raised his reddened, tearful eyes to met hers.

"No, no he didn't kill her. Her name is T'hane by the way. Although he felt as if he had somehow caused her death, he did not kill her. Oh God, he killed so many other people though as revenge for her death. No wonder his pain is so intense."

Kiri's voice sounded loud and clear in Hugh's head.

"Maybe now you understand a little better why it is so important for me to make amends for what I did, and why I have to give restitution for what I did and what I did not do."

I did. I really didn't know how anyone could live with that much emotional pain. I had only been exposed to it for about a couple of minutes but he had lived with it for, well who knows exactly, but a long time. At that moment I knew I had no choice but to help Kiri to find his peace and I knew that he had gone a long way toward doing that today in asking

88

T'hane, through Megan, to forgive him. I was feeling really shaky by this time and Megan looked none too strong either. Without speaking, we walked slowly back along the track towards the car. Megan's long skirt kept getting caught on the briars along the way and she would stop and untangle them carefully before proceeding. I hadn't noticed that happening on our way into the woods.

"Funny," Megan said, as she bent once again to release the material from the grasp of a small, yet vicious, thorn bush. "It seems the wood doesn't want me to leave."

As if to confirm her statement, she became more entangled in the next few steps and by now was becoming quite exasperated.

"Wait here," I said, and I took off back to the car.

In the boot I found an old blanket and carried back to where I had left Megan. Just before I got to her I spied a small clearing beneath the spread of a large beech and laid the blanket out there.

"Megan," I called, "make your way over here. Let's rest awhile before we go".

Megan had obviously managed to free herself and a moment or two later she found me sitting on the blanket waiting for her. Her face changed the moment she saw me. The smile had gone and I noticed a tension appear around her mouth and in the set of her jaw. I recognized this of old as a clear signal of her anger. She was staring at the blanket. What a fool! I knew exactly what she was thinking. She reckoned that this had all been an elaborate ploy on my part to get her out here, on her own, and seduce her. From her position I'd have thought the same thing. I kept my voice as calm and as even as I could.

"Come on Megan, just come and sit down. Look I'm not

going to try anything. Lets just sit here awhile and recover from what's happened. I'm still feeling pretty bad and I don't think I'm quite up to driving yet."

She moved towards me but I could still see suspicion in her eyes. I lay out on the blanket and looked up into the tree. It was huge. I imagined it spreading the protection of its branches over us so that nothing bad could happen to either of us ever again. It felt good. Slowly my body was returning to normal after Kiri's 'visit'. I looked up at Megan's back as she sat sentinel beside me. I raised my hand and began stroking her shoulders. She seemed tense and why wouldn't she be after what had just happened and what she perceived might yet happen. I just wanted to soothe her, to reassure. It seemed to be working, I could feel her soften and her breathing deepen. Eventually, resigned or reassured, I didn't know which, she lay down beside me, our hands lightly touching.

At that moment I believe a spell was woven around us in that wood. I felt complete connection and love for this woman. It was deep and mighty and eternal. We had loved an eternity and I knew that we always would and the feeling was as real and as solid as the earth that we lay on. I turned to look at her and in that same instant she turned to meet my gaze and a recognition took place. It was silent and pure and absolute. I felt complete. Something that I hadn't even known I'd lost had been found and all was now well with the world. I just knew that Megan felt the same. We smiled at one another and the pact was sealed. I knew we would see this thing through together. I didn't know how I just knew we would. As we lay there looking into each other's souls, I knew that I wanted this woman more than life but right at this moment I was going to do absolutely nothing about it, after all I had said I wouldn't hadn't I?

Megan was staring into Hugh's eyes, safe in the knowledge that no sexual encounter would be forthcoming,

90

and desperate for it all at the same time.

Hugh dropped her off with half an hour to spare before the kids came home from school. She felt flustered. It had been quite a day. A gnawing ache in her stomach reminded her that she had not eaten since breakfast and she put a piece of bread under the grill to toast. When she had eaten it, the gnawing in the pit of her stomach was still there and she realized that it had little to do with hunger, well not for food anyway. But in a way it was still hunger. Hunger for the deep connection that she felt with Hugh. Hunger for his body, but more than all this she realized that she was hungry for the spiritual contact that her relationship with Hugh sparked. Whilst she had known him the world had taken on new hues and dimensions. She had established a deep spiritual contact with the natural world which she had had as a child, fostered by her father, but that in the recent years had been absent. In fact in recent years she realized that she had been absent. Absent from life, just doing enough to get through the days, hiding her feelings of isolation and putting on a brave face when necessary. She supposed that it had been working but perhaps she hadn't really been fooling anyone. Hugh had certainly seen through it. What was she going to do? She began to feel desperate. What could she do? She had a husband, two children, a home, she couldn't walk away from all that. She would just have to accept that this was her lot and make the best of it.

The children arrived, tired and crotchety, and distracted her for the rest of the evening from any further soul searching. Jack arrived home at 10 p.m. and after a few cursory exchanges they went to bed. Lying there in the darkness beside his sleeping body, Megan had never felt so alone. In the early hours of the morning she had reached a decision. She needed Hugh in her life. She needed his friendship which was so nurturing and supportive. She couldn't continue as she had before, not having experienced something better. She couldn't go back. A new Megan was emerging and she felt she owed it to herself to encourage and support the fragile personality that now felt so real to her. She had questions too, lots of questions to put to Hugh. The visit to Batcombe had posed as many questions as it had answered and not least among them was the question about her own companion spirit. How come she wasn't having all these weird sensations that Hugh was experiencing? Hugh phoned the next morning and she was able to ask him.

"Hmm, I don't know but I guess I'm working with energy all the time now so there is more opportunity for these weird things to happen," Hugh responded.

"Well if this T'hane is going to use me in the way Kiri is using you shouldn't I see some evidence of it. It's clear what you are getting out of this strange relationship but what am I going to get from it?" Megan asked.

There was a pause from Hugh. He was listening for Kiri's voice in his head.

"Kiri says more than you can imagine, an understanding of the meaning of love."

Megan believed him and was immediately transported back to the session with Hugh when she had experienced such a powerful sensation of Divine Love. She was also reminded of the evening in the Tai Chi class when Hugh had suddenly asked her what it would mean to have someone say, "I love you," over and over again. She was brought abruptly back from this memory by the tone in Hugh's voice suddenly becoming very serious. He seemed to be asking her to be with him. He was telling her again that he loved her but with more intensity this time. Megan could feel her head swimming. Panic was rising in her.

"I can't Hugh, I just can't."

"I have to see you Megan, please at least let me see you."

The phone went dead.

I decided that I had to get away for a few days. There was a wonderful place that I had heard of a few hours drive away. It was a retreat that served good vegetarian food in a calm atmosphere and that had a fougou in the grounds. The fougou was a long underground passage that opened up into a cave. Whilst the origins of such a structure were obscure it seemed it was some kind of prehistoric shrine. The thought of going to ground for a while appealed immensely.

NIGHT VISIT

Megan was not feeling at all well. She didn't seem to have any energy and she was feeling very depressed. It was only now that she recognized the feeling of resignation deep inside her as a kind of depression. It even had a physical location she discovered, a black intense tennis ball sized emptiness in her solar plexus. However, she was convinced that what was bothering her now was Hugh. She had not been able to get him out of her head for days now. She was worried without knowing exactly why. She was also concerned about a dream that she had had the night before. Hugh had featured strongly in it and he seemed to be in a cave somewhere. She was really concerned. It had all seemed so real. She had a growing fear that he had done something stupid. That afternoon, against her better judgment, she picked up the phone and dialled his number. There was no reply. Shrugging off the feeling of unease she decided to venture out into the garden, which was always a special haven of hers, and tidy up a bit.

It didn't seem that there was much to do in the garden when she had started. But one thing lead to another and Megan realized that she had spent several hours just pottering, the sun warm on her back as she crouched or bent over the flower beds. The kids would want tea soon. There were just the three of them tonight, as usual at the weekends Jack was away. After tea they all sat around watching the television until it was time for bed. Megan had let the kids stay up later than she would normally have liked but she wanted the company and, once they were tucked up in bed, she decided to take a bath and have an early night herself.

The bath was most welcome. She eased her slightly aching limbs into the water and slid down until her chin was just level with the bubbles on the surface. She took a deep breath. The physical work in the garden had made her feel better and she always derived immense satisfaction from looking out at the neat and tended beds even at this time of year when most of their true glory was over. Sleep came easily as she slid between the sheets and as her head hit the pillow she was already drifting.

The world was silent when she was aroused a few hours later. She wasn't sure if she was really asleep or in that twilight zone between sleep and wakefulness. She still had her eyes closed but what had awakened her, if indeed she was awake, was the pressure on her body. Someone, she could hear their breathing, was lying on her. It wasn't unpleasantly heavy but she was aware of not being able to move. Then her body began to rock gently. Swirls of pleasure arose from deep in her abdomen and trickled out through her entire body. At first she assumed that Jack had returned and was making love with her. Not likely, she thought. She had never felt the sensations that she was experiencing now before. Catching her breath she was suddenly taken by surprise as the sea of sensations grew to a crescendo and then swept her away with a flood of sweet ecstatic release. Her eyes flew wide open and she pushed herself rapidly up the bed to a sitting position. Staring rapidly around the darkened room, she registered the fact that she was quite alone!

Well that was quite a dream, she thought as she slid beneath the covers once more. Turning on her side, she couldn't help smiling to herself. The next morning she tried phoning Hugh again. There was still no reply.

After the children had gone off to school on Monday morning, Megan began her Tai Chi practice. Her body felt heavy again though and the nagging worry of the least few days had returned with a vengeance. She decided to skip practice. She would try Hugh's number again. She found herself wrestling madly with her conscience. She should just let him be. She didn't have to phone. She was a grown woman after all she had the strength to resist these foolish impulses. Even as she wrestled with these thoughts, her hand, trance like, was dialling his number. Maybe this companion spirit of hers was having more influence than she realized.

He sounded sleepy as he answered the phone. His voice was even deeper and more husky than usual. She could tell that she had woken him. The words tumbled from her mouth. She hadn't known exactly what she wanted to say to him as she dialled his number and she was none too clear even now.

"Where have you been?" she asked, knowing that it was none of her business but that it was vitally important to her all the same.

"I've been trying to get hold of you all weekend. I feel dreadful and it has something to do with you. I dreamed you were in a cave or something. I thought something dreadful must have happened to you."

"I'm okay," I said, once I'd come to and figured out where I was. "I've been away for a few days, but you're right, I was in a cave of sorts."

There was along pause. After the initial rush of words it now seemed that Megan had nothing more to say.

"Look," I said. "I've only been in bed a few hours. It took me longer to drive back than I had anticipated. I'll speak to you later."

"Okay," said Megan, "sorry for waking you."

Hugh dropped the phone back on the receiver.

Megan heard the click in her ear. God, she thought, is

there no way that I can break away from this man. In her heart she realized that the answer to this was an emphatic NO! When Hugh phoned sometime later they arranged to meet at the Centre the next day.

POINT OF NO RETURN

 I was scared. Megan was arriving at two and I had not been able to focus on any else the whole day. I had made up my mind that I could no longer keep this relationship on a purely friendship basis. There was a growing sexual attraction between us and it was becoming unbearable. I had held back at Batcombe even though she had looked so beautiful that day, a turquoise oasis in the forest green, but she had to be willing to take this relationship a stage further as well. She was the one with commitments after all. I felt like an adolescent as I opened the door to her. She stepped into the hall and looked around nervously.

"Coffee?" I asked, my voice sounding a little too tight for my liking.

"Great," she said.

I walked into the kitchen and she followed me. There was silence whilst I made the drink. We took it into the lounge to drink it and the conversation was stilted and pretty general. We were acting like a couple of strangers instead of people who had known each other for years. It was obvious that I had to be the one to make the first move but it wasn't coming easily. I could feel my mouth go dry. What if she stormed out, what if she refused to see me again, what if she was deeply offended, what if? I was prevaricating. There was a chance that any of the aforementioned could happen and maybe even something that I hadn't even covered but what the hell, I had to do it. I took a breath and stepped off the precipice. What would be would be.

"You know I want you Megan," I began.

She nodded and looked down at her lap. I waited for the protestations to begin. They didn't.

"I love you and I want to be with you." I said.

I reached out and cupped my hand around her chin. She raised her head and looked at me. It was impossible to read her face but it looked quiet and serene. She nodded again. It felt like an acknowledgement so I decided to proceed. I leaned towards her and kissed her on the mouth. I felt her mouth soften in response. I kissed her again, this time more urgently, my tongue exploring to see if it would be received by her slightly quivering mouth. She surged towards me and we embraced. Locked together, I was instantly erect. I wanted her now at this moment, but I knew I had to reign myself in. I was overwhelmed by the strength of my reaction to her and I momentarily drew back. Moving slowly, I started to remove her clothing as we continued to explore each others mouths.

It seemed to be happening in slow motion, a slow rhythmic dance, as our movements coordinated naturally together. It seemed to take along time and I was struck by the paradox of wanting desperately to be inside her and yet equally desperate for these moments to never end. Then she was naked. For the first time I drew back and looked at her. She had a delicious body with wide shoulders and full breasts. Her hips were accentuated by a narrow waist and her legs long. She was beautiful. I was still fully clothed and I felt suddenly awkward sitting there staring at her nakedness. I pulled the throw from the sofa and wrapped it around her shoulders. It draped around her and fell in folds on the floor. She made no effort to pull it tight around her and through the gap in the material I still could glimpse her. It made her even more tantalising to me. Slowly I started to undress. Slowly because I didn't want to give her the impression I was desperate, even though I was, but also because I was suddenly feeling apprehensive. It's a common enough feeling for men I guess, that moment before you actually move in for the kill as it were. It's a really vulnerable place to be. You are calling all the shots and what if you are calling them wrong. You are also laying yourself wide open for comparison and even criticism. Hell, this woman was no virgin. How would I add up to her other sexual experiences. I didn't know what she was used to. However, with my cock eager to do business there was no time for negotiation. Standing there before her, matching her nakedness, I waited for the signal, you know the one that says it's alright. I looked at Megan. Her eyes were on my groin taking note of my obvious enthusiasm, then she slowly raised them to meet my gaze and smiled. That was it!

There had been no foreplay other than our playful tongues in each others mouth but I slid into her like a hot knife through butter. She was as ready as I was. I was content to just rest inside her, grateful for the acceptance and the feeling of deep connection. We kissed more. She ran her fingers down my back and over the mounds of my buttocks. Her touch was smooth like silk. I wrestled my mouth away from hers and nuzzled into her neck whilst my pelvis began to move gently against her. It felt so easy, so familiar. I wanted to be gentle with her. I could feel her body moving in rhythm to mine with that same easy connection that had been there right from the first few months of our friendship. It was still exerting itself here now. Our bodies seemed familiar to each other. There was no embarrassment. My body knew what it had to do to please her and her body knew likewise. I could feel myself slipping into an altered state of consciousness. I was filled with the scent and the feel of her. There was nothing else, nothing in the world. I became total self absorbed in the experience. The touch of her hand on my face brought me back to the lounge. I opened my eyes and looked into Megan's again.

"You see, I knew you would remember me," she said and

smiled widely.

I smiled back and withdrew from her slowly. It was done. We had stepped over the boundary of our old relationship and there was no going back. Neither one of us had climaxed. It had not seemed necessary. It was as if sex had merely been the vehicle for a deeper connection between us. We dressed immediately and I went to make more coffee.

"What did you mean," I said when she came into the kitchen after a few minutes.

"When?"

"A moment ago. You said you knew I would remember you. What did you mean?" I asked.

"Oh that! Well when we introduced ourselves to you in that first Tai Chi class you said that you wouldn't remember anyone's name because they never usually stuck at it long enough," Megan responded.

"Yeah, I always say that and it's true, people are always looking for a quick fix, hoping to get something quickly. Tai Chi looks so easy when you see someone performing it they don't realize the dedication it takes for it to look that easy." I said, getting back on to an old hobby horse of mine.

"Right, well on that evening I said to myself you'll remember my name and it came into my head again just now. If you believe Kiri's story then it gives the phrase an even deeper meaning doesn't it?" Megan asked.

TWO EDGED SWORD

Christmas was only a few days away and Megan was dreading it. Normally she loved this time of year but this year she was wracked with conflicting emotions that were beginning to take their toll on her health. She had grown frighteningly thin, her appetite having slipped away with the excess pounds. Food landed heavy in her stomach and some mornings she practically gagged as she tried to consume breakfast. She wasn't sure how long she could continue in this way. Running around after presents wasn't helping much either and she had no heart for the coming festivities.

On Christmas Eve she left Jack and the kids at home and set off to collect the vegetables from town. She had left early so as to beat the crowds. It was a vain attempt, everyone else having the same idea. She shouldered her way into the greengrocers and battled the other customers to fill her basket. There were a few other items that she needed to collect; paper napkins, some gold candles and gold coated sugared almonds for the table decorations. Jack's parents along with her mother and father were going to be with them for Christmas lunch and she wanted to make the effort to make everything right. God, everything right, how could everything ever be right again! She realized that she was unduly concerned about making this Christmas as good a celebration as possible if only to cement the feeling of family and gloss over the fact that all was not well with Jack and her. She had not intended to see Hugh but as she locked the boot of the car after putting the last of her shopping inside she felt compelled to pay him just a short visit. She would not be able to have any contact with him at all over the Christmas period and she wanted to see him one more time.

She rang the doorbell and waited. There was a cold wind snaking round the corner of the building and cutting into her through the heavy coat she was wearing. She shivered and pulled the collar tighter around her throat. She could hear no sound from inside the house and rang the bell again. Resigned to the fact that he was probably not in she turned to go when her ears picked up the click of the door handle on the inner door in the hallway. A minute later Hugh stood framed in the doorway. He had obviously just got out of bed to answer the door. He looked sleepy and pulled his dressing gown tightly around him as he encountered the chill wind. He was smiling widely and inviting her in out of the cold. He turned and began walking up the stairs in front of her. Megan followed.

"I'm glad you came," Hugh said. "I've got something for you."

Megan was intrigued. It had not occurred to her to bring anything for Hugh. He walked in front of her. She was clipping at his heels like a small dog. He climbed the three flights of stairs to his bedroom and sat down heavily on the bed. Megan sat down beside him.

"I am so glad you came," Hugh repeated and kissed her lightly on the cheek.

"Me too" said Megan "I hadn't intended to but..." she looked at him and grinned.

He hugged her hard to him and they were content to just be close.

Suddenly Hugh broke free and stood up.

"Come over here," he said, "and kneel down on the rug."

"What?" Megan replied.

"You heard. Just kneel down and close your eyes."

Megan had no idea what he was up to but she knew that she had little time here with him and she didn't want to waste it in fruitless argument. She raised herself from the bed and knelt on the rug as directed. She gave him a long hard look before she consented to bow her head and close her eyes. She heard Hugh move across the room and open the wardrobe. He was obviously taking something from it.

"Okay. You can open your eyes now" she heard him say.

Megan glanced down at a roll of green silk on the floor in front of her. It was about a three feet long and she had no idea what it held. Hugh was giving nothing away he was just standing looking at her, waiting for her reaction. Megan leaned forward and began to unravel the silk. She took hold of each end and began to lift it slowly. When she had raised the material almost up to her eye level the content of the wrap fell free on the rug. Moving the silk to one side and placing in on the floor beside her she looked down at the sword in front of her. She gave a small gasp.

"You'll need one to practice the sword form," Hugh said. "It's about time that you took your Tai Chi practice into the weapons training."

Megan stared at the sword. She was delighted and surprised at the present. Her Tai Chi meant so much to her and that made the gift even more special, but as she stared at the clean lines of the sword she was overwhelmed with emotion. The sword suddenly took on a powerful symbolic meaning. She felt that if she leaned forward and picked it up, accepted it, she would literally and figuratively be taking up the sword. It seemed to symbolize the battle ahead, a fight that she and Hugh would have to fight together. She was suddenly frightened. She doubted that Hugh saw his gift as anything more than a obvious gift to martial artist but it loomed large in her psyche as an object of great power, signifying a monumental challenge that she wasn't sure she was up to.

Once she accepted this then there would be no turning back. Had she the courage to pick it up? In what seemed an eternity of time Megan stared at the sword. She reached out her fingers and traced them along the swords length then with a swift intake of breath she picked it up. There it was done!

"Thank you, Hugh," she said. "You don't know what this means to me."

At that moment in time neither Hugh nor Megan could have been aware of just how significant that moment was to be in their lives. Both their lives at that moment were indeed balanced on that sword's edge, and which way they would move, on which side they would come down was still at that moment unknown.

When she got home Megan tucked the gift away in the bottom of her wardroom under her sweaters and set to work to create the perfect Christmas. How she got through the three days of Christmas she didn't know. Of course she was kept busy and that helped. Jack was being distant, or was it her whose mind was elsewhere so that he appeared distant. They snapped at each other and the children a lot. Jack was even bad-tempered with his parents. Megan hoped that no one would notice, or if they did that they would put it down to the stress of cooking and organizing. She was glad when both sets of parents departed and there were just the four of them again. She hadn't realized until that moment what a pressure she had felt just having them around.

She made some tea and handed a cup to Jack who was sitting in front of the television. She took her cup and sat at the opposite side of the room. As she put the cup down on the table she moved the set of Christmas snap shots that Grandpa had left to one side to accommodate it. On impulse she picked them up and began leafing through them. Like most instant photos the quality wasn't superb but the images that stared back at her were clear enough. In each frame she seemed to be set slightly apart from everyone else. She looked thin and gaunt and seemed to be staring off into space at some unknown future. My God, she though to herself, I have to do something. I can't go on like this.

A few days later she told Jack that she wanted to leave. She was distraught. She loved this man. He was a good man and he had looked after her and the kids well. But she couldn't reach him, couldn't communicate with him and without that contact, without a deep connection, she knew she would shrivel up and die inside. Hell, it was happening already and Jack hadn't even noticed! He was probably busy doing his own shrivelling. She explained as much to Jack through heavy sobs. He didn't understand. He was hurt and angry and confused and she couldn't blame him. Of course immediately he wanted to know if there was someone else and she couldn't lie to him. The pain for both of them was unbearable.

INFORMATION OVERLOAD

I could feel my heart physically stop as I heard Megan's voice on the other end of the phone line.

"I've done it Hugh. I've told Jack. If you still want me I'm yours."

It was seven o'clock in the evening. I had come in just twenty minutes or so earlier from a cold, inhospitable world of raw January weather. I had stuck a couple of potatoes in the oven to bake and was curled up on the sofa trying to stay awake as the warm atmosphere of the sitting room began to combat the chill in my body. When the phone rang I expected it to be a client. Megan was the last voice I expected to hear and her news brought me up sharp, my dulled senses suddenly alert and heightened.

"Of course I do," I heard myself say.

I hoped that my voice didn't betray the panic I was feeling. My fantasies of the last year were about to come true but I wasn't sure that I could actually cope with the reality. Apart from the huge emotional adjustment that I would have to make there were practical considerations that had to be taken care of. I couldn't just move Megan and her children into my place, assuming she wouldn't leave them, without making extra bedrooms. The rooms were there of course, that was one thing I had plenty of, but they were hardly furnished in a way that kids would find acceptable. I expressed my concerns to Megan.

"Give me a week or so," I said. "I have to get a couple of single beds and some cupboards and bedding. I just need a little time."

I registered the disappointment in Megan's voice.

"Okay," she said, "I can't speak anymore now. I'll phone again tomorrow when I'm on my own. Bye, Hugh."

By the time I sat down on the sofa again I was sweating. It wasn't that hot in the house so I surmised that it was fear that was causing the reaction. I could feel the panic rising in me again. Oh God! I had to get a grip! I supposed that I had never really believed that she would leave. Talk about 'wish for what you want but be very sure that you want it' or what ever that phrase was that people were fond of quoting. Well, whether I thought that Megan would come or not was immaterial now. She was, and if she had had her way she would have been on my doorstep right now. I could understand her hurry. I could only guess at the courage it must have taken to talk with Jack and how desperately uncomfortable it must be for all of them at this moment. Still I had meant what I said and I really did need the few days of grace to prepare, not just the house but, as I realized with dawning candour, myself.

I spent the next few days in a whirl of activity. I busied myself sorting, organising, shopping; indeed anything, in fact, that would take my mind from the enormity of the event that was about to occur. There was not enough time for my mind to calm down, but nine days after Megan's initial call, there I was ushering them into the house and hoping to God that all of them would settle and be alright here. I knew it wasn't going to be easy. Megan and I spoke long into the wee small hours about our fears and concerns. She cried a lot. I managed to put on a brave face and maintain an air of calm and certainty in the face of her bewilderment. As she undressed for bed that night, I took a long hard look at her and was suddenly devastated by what I saw. Her slim body was now skin and bone. She looked frightened and vulnerable. I held

110

out my arms to her as I lay on the bed and she curled up inside them like a cat, her knees drawn tight to her chest and her head buried in my shoulder. I tried to comfort her, make everything alright. I wanted to take away her hurt and make everything right for her but I knew that was impossible. The best I could do was be strong for her and hold her and make her safe until time alone started to heal the wounds. We lay huddled together in the dark like children afraid that the boogie man might find us. I felt so desperately alone. I wasn't sure that I could get Megan through this by myself.

"Oh, God help us," I whispered.

Almost as soon as Megan and I were together the strange happenings and Kiri's intrusion in our lives became more and more obvious. I was reminded of his words about having to wait until my resistances were low before I would allow him in. Well certainly my defences were well and truly down at this moment. All my spare energy when I wasn't treating people went into caring for Megan. Her sadness was overwhelming. I did everything I could to get her to lighten up. I didn't know I could come up with so many silly voices and antics in order to get her to break onto a smile. I played the clown like never before and certainly never since. Sometimes it would work, sometimes the enormity of what she had done and what life might now hold for her was just too heavy to lift. Most evenings I cooked a meal for us both and watched as she painfully and slowly placed a small quantity into her mouth before protesting that it was delicious but she just couldn't eat much. Later on I would run her a bath before we both fell into bed locked together in the grip of uncertainty.

After a few weeks or so something strange began happening. As Megan sat on the settee one evening she suddenly said she was overcome with tiredness. I wasn't unduly surprised. Her energy was low anyway. As she looked across the room at me she suddenly began staring intently.

"Oh God, Hugh," she said, "your face is changing again."

As I looked back at her, her eyelids became heavy and she succumbed to what I thought was sleep. For a moment I just sat and watched her. I was still marvelling at the fact that she was here in my life. Then surprisingly she began to speak. Her eyes were still closed and her voice was slow and ponderous. As I watched, her face took on a quizzical expression as if she were trying to make sense of what she was saying. Pretty soon I realized that she was conveying information and although it was her speaking it wasn't really her. When she wasn't clear I would question her and she would wait until she received an answer before replying. This was the first time that both she and I had seen any evidence of Kiri's statement that Megan, too, had a companion spirit. It was our assumption that it was indeed her that Megan was channelling. In Megan's present exhausted state, T'hane had found a way through. As quickly as her eyes had closed in the first instance, Megan gave a shudder and her eyes were suddenly wide open. The atmosphere in the room was thick with energy and charged with a golden light. Megan commented on it.

"Goodness. That was weird," she said. "I felt like I was someone else but at the same time I knew that I was really me sitting here in the lounge. Can you see what's happened to the room?"

"That's what I've been experiencing with Kiri," I responded. "I still feel like me most of the time, but he is somehow a part of me, also, and sometimes he just takes over for a while."

"Exactly," Megan replied, "but what's going on? What's this all about?"

"I only know what Kiri told me and I relayed to you. He

and this woman have some sort of unfinished business and they have 'chosen' you and me to help sort it out for them."

A set pattern began to emerge after this first experience of Megan's. During the day we were left pretty much alone. I got on with the sessions I had to give and Megan got on with getting the kids to school and holding down her small part-time job that she had held on to after leaving Jack. It was the only bit of her old life that she had kept. Megan was slowly regaining her strength and the kids had, with difficulty, settled into the new routine. Heaven knows what they made of everything but they were coping, albeit by retreating into the safety of their rooms and spending most of their time interacting with each other and the television set. Kiri kept telling me that they would be okay and to just give them time. I relayed his words to Megan at the times when she was overcome with remorse about the effects of her actions on them.

Some evenings Megan would slip into her trance state which was always preceded by the shift in the atmosphere in the room. The thick golden light always heralded the channelling. It was at night however that things would become very different indeed. Megan and I would settle for the night and within a few minutes we would hear the cry of an owl. The first time we heard it we could hardly believe our ears. The house was in the centre of town, hardly owl territory, and yet here we were definitely hearing the cry of an owl. At first it was just a weird occurrence but soon we came to recognize that it signalled the beginning of some kind of episode for us, for night after night would come the eerie cry. We would get into bed and turn out the light and wait. It was never long in coming, the long plaintive note filling the room with the tinge of sadness. At the owl's command, first one of us would go into a deep trance state and begin accessing all sorts of information and then, just to be fair, the next night it would be the other one's turn. Night after night the owl came without fail, the insistent call urging us to go back and seek out more and more information. We were told after a while that to make the induction process easier we should lie on our backs with our left hand palm up and the right palm down. It seemed to work. Soon we got to the stage where the owl's call became the signal for one of us to assume this position and almost immediately either Kiri or T'hane would come through.

At first the experience was disjointed and to be honest we couldn't make much sense of it. The sheer presence of these beings was always accompanied by huge energetic shifts, which made the process often extremely uncomfortable. Our minds struggled to cope with the vast amount of information that was being poured in to us at a phenomenal rate. On one occasion Megan began burning up, her body shaking madly as she struggled with the intensity of what was occurring.

"I feel like I'm dying," she kept muttering, as I held her as tightly as I could to contain her energy.

It felt as if both our bodies were being rewired in someway in order to take the extra voltage that was being pumped through them. I had no real way of knowing what was really going on. The voice in my head, the information I accessed, my face changing—when these had first occurred I had put it down to a psychotic episode on my part. But now here was another human being who verified the physical shifts and who could also have conversations with Kiri just as easily as I could. Megan's reality and mine were becoming fused. When we became these other beings everything around us changed. It was like living in a parallel universe where the two of us were stronger, more energetically aware and more intensely connected than we could have thought possible in our everyday reality.

The deep trance sessions seemed to vary in length but when it was over we were always high. We had so much energy we didn't know what to do with it. Well we did, at least it didn't take much imagination to figure out that sex was a great way of using up the excess. Sometimes as we lay with each other we were aware that it wasn't us that were joined, but Kiri and T'hane. They often took the opportunity to connect physically again through the medium of our bodies. It was a privilege to feel the deep telepathic connection between them and the intense attraction which of course rubbed off on us. Often we made love for hours, passionately, tenderly, intensely. When we at last separated and returned to our normal state of consciousness from the surreal space that we had been operating in we were always intensely happy. Indeed, at these times Megan was more present and bright than at any other. Our nightly rituals were always finished off with hot toast and jam with tea at about four in the morning.

This went on night after night for weeks. The few hours of sleep that we managed to grab seemed to be sufficient for our needs and even during the day we had more than enough energy to get done what was needed. The whole thing was surreal. Gradually over time we began to make sense of what was going on. We were receiving information about these two people's lives. Well, not just receiving the information but reliving it with all its pain, all its drama and all its ecstasy. Through all its intensity what both Megan and I experienced constantly was an overwhelming sense of love from these beings. Love for each other, love for us and over and above all this a powerful and Divine Love that stood alone and apart from the drama of all our lives. We felt supported and aided in the process that we found ourselves in. Eventually over many nights the whole story of Kiri and T'hane life unfolded and it became abundantly clear why it was so important to Kiri to get his message across.

ONCE UPON A TIME IN A FAR OFF LAND

Kiri had never known his blood family. He had vague recollections of a face set with two dark pools of inky blackness and swirling frond like patterns covering the cheeks and chin. It was a powerful image, yet he got a warm feeling in the pit of his stomach when he closed his eyes and tried to bring it back into sharper focus. But all he knew, really knew, was the old man beside him. He turned his gaze toward him now and studied the strong profile of the man crouched beside him on the beach gutting fish. His body, though old, still had a power about it. His dark skin was tanned black across his shoulders, except for a strange scar on the right one. Kiri knew nothing of the man's history before he came to live with him and all Uncle would say about the scar was that it was from a spear wound sustained in his youth. The scar had healed badly and now formed an ugly raised patch that had turned white and crusty over time. His old fingers worked the bone knife in his hand with practiced skill. As he gutted, a low chant escaped his lips. He was oblivious to all around him as he gave the small lifeless body in his hand his complete attention. Wrapping it in a ti leaf, he laid it carefully across the twigs braced across the embers of the fire, rocked back on his heels and throwing back his head called out in a loud sonorous voice.

Kiri turned his gaze towards the ocean and after several minutes, during which the old man kept up the chant, a black fin appeared in the water off to his right and made its way slowly across the bay. Kiri watched the familiar ritual. The fin would make several passes in front of them and then, with a rush, the shark's head would appear above the surface and its sleek body would rise and turn in the air before plunging to the sea again. On some occasions this would be repeated several times but tonight, just once. His shiny body silhouetted against the gold of the setting sun and the diamond drops of water falling after him before the sea became calm once more.

Yes, the old man was the only family, friend, companion that Kiri had ever known. He had been told by those who travelled the great ocean from his homeland with him in his youth, that he was an outcast, sent out from his mother and father at an early age. But Uncle had told him another story. That he was special. Marked with the sign of the gods at his birth, his family had been fearful of his power and the suspicious eyes of the neighbours and so had given him over to the care and protection of their Kahuna kuni ola who had argued both the boy's, and the gods' case and won. This revered old man was trained in the art of 'anā'anā, the art of sorcery and magic. He specialized in divining the source of the 'anā'anā, or death spell, perpetrated on a victim and then saving and avenging the same. This made him much respected and feared in the community, for it was a well known fact that if you had a difficult task to be done a Kahuna skilled in the arts of both black and white magic was the most powerful and often the most successful. And so it was that Kiri began to study the ways of his mentor and the rituals for the creation of magic. The task was not an easy undertaking. He was among, other things, required to eat certain plants that contained poisonous substances that brought him to his knees and made him retch again and again. But they took him to the realm of the 'aumakua and he was able to know the ways of the gods and converse directly with them. In learning the pule 'anā'anā, he was also required to gain control over his emotions in order to contain and focus the power of the magic and especially to learn to control his not inconsiderable temper. This Kiri found especially hard and was thankful that his life took him infrequently in contact with the villagers

118

who could readily ignite the spark of his passion. His life was consecrated to the gods. Everything that he owned, meagre though it was—his food, water gourd, his house—were all hallowed. He belonged to the gods. He was their servant and he was ruled by them.

Kiri rose and walked to the water's edge. He was not tall but his dark skinned body was lithe and fit, and why wouldn't it be? He swam daily with the dolphins and the turtles. They were his friends. He could converse with them and they with him. These things he had learnt from Uncle. His long black hair brushed across his shoulders, for he was forbidden to cut it, and his face, turned towards the sun, was strong with high cheek bones and a long, flattened nose. It was only when he turned and the golden light glanced off the contours and ridges of his face, turning it to burnished bronze, that the blood mark on his forehead became noticeable.

These last few days had been busy for both of them. The time of the thanksgiving was almost upon them. A great feast had to be prepared to commemorate the life and the health of the body and for all the help received from the gods. All work ceased at this time and it was part of Uncle's responsibilities to make sure that all pig, coconut and fish were kept kapu at this time, for the eating of all flesh foods was forbidden. The fish baking slowly in the ti leaf was to be the last for them for the next three months. Kiri enjoyed this time of the year. People were relaxed and happy as all work ceased and they came together to feast and talk. Young men wrestled good naturedly during the day and rode the high waves for fun instead of engaging in the search for fish. At dusk, when the moon wove her own special blend of magic, men and women would lie with each other. The young, fondling and exploring each other's bodies with giggles and gasps, and the more experienced rolling, locked together in embrace at the waters edge, rising and falling like the ocean herself. For Kiri, the knowledge of women was forbidden him and his arousal had to be kept as hidden as the knowledge his uncle imparted to him. He lived on the outskirts of humanity. Half man, half god, and on nights such as this the man was winning and he felt the ache in his loins and his breath catch in his chest.

As the warm waters lapped his feet he noticed a woman stumbling, half walking, half running across the sand toward the hut. He knew what that meant. He had seen it many times before. He could feel her anguish mingled with hot anger even before she blundered past him and up to the old man. Kiri closed his eyes and took a deep breath and released the tension from his chest and sex. He turned and walked up to where the woman and Uncle were engaged in low conversation. She thrust a small piece of tapa cloth into Uncle's hand and turned to weave her way back across the beach. Uncle unwrapped the cloth with tender care, peeling back the corners like the skin of a banana. In the bowl of his hand lay a blood encrusted finger. He raised his eyes and he and Kiri's eyes and spirit locked together as did their jaws to seal the unspoken pact. There was work to be done and it was always dangerous, always uncertain. Any work that involved the death spell held an inherent risk. They worked on the knife-edge of life and death where one careless manoeuvre could be their last. They walked in silence to the heiau to pray for the protection of the gods and the success of their work the next day.

They took an offering of 'awa with them, which they laid before the high stone in the centre of the heiau, for it was well known that this was a favourite of the gods. Kiri looked around him at the square laid out before them, bounded on all sides by walls of carefully selected and crafted stones. He turned his attention to the tower of long branches to his left from where the priest kahuna would speak to the people, now standing empty. Reverently he drew his eyes to the carved face of the god nearest him. Large empty eyes stared back at him from above its wide grimacing mouth. Kiri felt a small river of fear run the length of his back.

It took several minutes for both men to settle their bodies and focus their mind to the task at hand. Uncle began the breathing. In the quiet night air Kiri heard him take the first long, slow intake of breath. This was his queue to begin. For almost thirty minutes both men deepened their breathing until they felt their chests would burst. Their heads throbbed as the blood pounded in their skulls and then, from somewhere in the depths of each man's belly, an energy began to build. Each man allowed his mana, his life force, to build steadily over the next minutes. Kiri could feel the air around them grow thick and chill, and as the energy of powerful emotion filled his body, he fought to keep control as his eyes misted over. In his mind he focused on the 'aumakua who was to help them. Somehow he had to contain this power. It was rising from the earth, filling him, filling him so completely he was aware of nothing else. Then, without any visible signal, as one, both he and Uncle allowed the rush of energy to surge through them, hot and molten as Pele's volcanic fire. The night air cracked with the first syllable of the chant. The endless days and nights that Kiri had spent memorizing the prayers allowed them to spill from his lips without hesitation and the heiau resounded to the vibration of the prayers. In two hours it was done.

The next day Kiri prepared the fire on the beach. He had spent some time collecting fresh green leaves and branches for, it was crucial that the fire be lit with, and only consist of, green wood. One by one, and in small groups, the villagers arrived to stand silently around it. Word spreads like disease through a small community. Before the disbelieving eyes of the crowd, Kiri magically ignited the fire and the first small column of smoke lifted into the air. When all had assembled Uncle appeared. He had spent the morning in silent prayer and drinking the creamy liquid of the 'awa root to open his eyes and his mind to the spirits. Slowly he took the small piece of cloth that held the woman's gruesome offering. Lifting it above his head, he prayed for the gods to show him who had caused the death of her man. Then with a swift downward stroke of his arm he threw the finger into the fire. There was a short involuntary intake of breath from the small crowd. They had witnessed this before and knew what was to come.

There was a calm. Then, racing in across the ocean, the wind skidded to a halt on the beach whipping up sand into the faces of the assembly. The sky grew angry and black and, far off, thunder rumbled and complained bitterly at being woken. Suddenly a gentle misty rain began to fall on the beach. It was after this aspect of the phenomenon that Kiri had been named. As the gentle rain washed the faces of the crowd, out of the inky sky, a rainbow arc appeared. The gods had heard and had answered! A bolt of lightening crackled in the electrified air and struck the ground at Uncle's feet. The crowd was caught between its desire to run and the paralysis brought about by fear of the gods. For several minutes Uncle watched the billowing smoke from the fire and then, suddenly possessed by an unseen force, fell to the ground and began to writhe on the sand, shouting and foaming at the mouth. He called out to every god he felt he could muster. It was frightening to see. After a while he recovered and stood shakily to his feet. He turned to a small group of young men standing a little behind the main crowd.

"The gods have revealed him to me," he said, "and his name is—Makea."

"His name has been spoken aloud before all of you. He has been named by the gods and it will come to pass that on the third day of the new moon he, too, shall be taken from this life and the manner of his passing will be known by the Menehune."

And so it was that on the second day after the new moon, Makea was crushed by a suddenly avalanche of rock brought

122

on by torrential rains. The Menehune, the rock people, skilled in the working of stone, called to the spirits of the rock to help them lift the enormous stones as they uncovered his body. He died the following day.

The day after such a ceremony was usually a day of rest for Kiri and Uncle. The whole process had taken a great deal of their personal mana and they needed time to rebuild it. Kiri knew that there would be no instruction that day; besides he had a growing sense that the time of his initiation was near. Uncle had taught him almost all that he knew. This knowledge also included the gift of healing and the ability to read the clouds and so foretell the weather and even, to some extent, control the natural elements. Today the sky was clear except for the low cloud over the mountain. It would rain later and the large ring present around the moon last night foretold of storms to come, but for the moment there was calm and time to sit and eat from the bowl of poi on the table. The taro had been cooked a few days previously and then peeled with the sharp edge of a 'opihi shell. It had then been pounded on the poi board with a stone dipped regularly in water until it had become a thick, heavy paste. The paste had been wrapped in ti leaves and left until this morning, when a little of it had been mixed with water to become a thinner paste. It was fresh and sweet. Kiri ate well. He felt the hunger gnawing at his insides and relished the growing fullness in his belly. Uncle had already eaten and so he finished the bowl. It would soon spoil anyhow and become sour so he felt justified in licking around the bowl to gain every last morsel.

He had hoped for a quiet day but the gods had other ideas. In this small community kahuna were rare, and he and Uncle found themselves called upon to perform many tasks. Uncle left shortly after breakfast to see to a young boy who had broken his leg whilst climbing on the lava flows. He had gathered up a large bunch of the morning glory root from the Koali bush to treat the break and walked off saying he would return by noon. By mid-morning Kiri had been summoned to the house of a young woman writhing with the pain of childbirth. It was her first child and the labour had been continuing throughout the previous night to no avail. Her man and her mother fussed around her anxiously and looked up in relief when Kiri entered the hut. He knelt beside the woman and ran his practiced hands over her belly and between her legs. The baby was at the door ready to be born but fear and the over anxious attentions of her mother and husband had made the woman fitful and tense. He had brought the discarded leaves of the morning glory left behind by Uncle and he began crushing them in his hands and rubbing them over the woman's belly. He began the prayers to his own 'aumakua, the shark, and to the family 'aumakua of the woman. As he began the prayers, the woman began to wail and shout for the baby to be taken from inside her. Her husband danced around her distraught. Kiri took his hands from the woman's belly and rose to his feet. Walking up to the man he took him by the shoulders. The man froze coming back out of the fear trance he was in and Kiri, muttering under his breath, put his hand on the man's stomach. He immediately screamed in pain and fell to his knees gasping and panting. Kiri returned to the woman who had, at the same instant, fallen quiet and seemed almost sleepy. For the rest of the labour the man carried his wife's pain as she calmly let her son slip from her body. Kiri always had to smile at the poor man's surprise at finding himself the recipient of the birth pains instead of his wife. He could, of course, have taken the woman's pain himself but it was so much more entertaining this way. He cut the cord and massaged the woman's abdomen until the afterbirth was delivered. Carrying the blood-laden tissue outside to the nearby stream he washed it thoroughly in the running water. Carrying it back inside he bade the husband take it and bury it under a nearby tree, and with the new family now settled he made his way home. Uncle had not yet returned.

Most of Kiri's days were spent thus, either in learning or practice of the prayers and chants of his trade until he was word perfect, or in tending to the sick. Fortunately the previous day's ceremony was becoming something of a rarity. He was now confident of his skills and his ability to command the spiritual mana necessary for the tasks that he had to perform although he was aware that Uncle rarely entrusted the most difficult of cases to him. However, only at the last full moon he had been called to attend to a man near to death. The man was delirious with fever and open sores were appearing all over his body. Uncle had been unable to go with him and Kiri found himself alone and required to exact a cure on the man.

At first he had thought that it was the death spell again, that the man had been cursed by another Kahuna. He had no wish to perform the ceremony on his own. Instinct told him, however, that in this case it was not applicable. He decided to build a imu loa and set about instructing the family on how to dig out a trench the length of the man and line it with stones. He pointed out the kind of stones to the helpers so that they would choose those that would not break and splinter in intense heat. Along the bottom of the trench he laid a fire and for some time tended it until the stones glowed red. Onto the fire he laid green banana leaves and aromatic herbs until there was a lush bed of foliage which he instructed the man to lie upon. Covering him over with more banana leaves and earth, he instructed the family to leave him there with only water to refresh him for five days. Then he left. As he walked away he knew that the man would rise from the smouldering bed, his fever gone and his skin like a baby's.

Seven cycles of the moon later, Kiri was to build another imu. This time it was to hold the body of a pig for the 'ailolo ceremony—the ceremony that would see him a fully fledged Kahuna. Kiri was the second of Uncle's pupils. Most Kahunas had three or four such pupils in their lifetime, although Kiri

125

somehow doubted that the old man would take another.

The preparation of the imu was crucial to his success as a Kahuna and he spent three days and nights fasting, drinking only a little salt water to purge and cleanse his system. He picked the best stones that he could find, all of them roughly the size of his palm. As he laid them in the pit he prayed to his ancestors, the sharks, and to the ancestors of his family, wherever they were and asked them to bless the initiation. He laid the green branches in the base of the pit and once again miraculously they burst into flame at his insistence. The pig he had chosen had already been slaughtered and gutted. With a sharp edge of his 'opihi shell he sliced off the tip of the snout, and then the ears, which he finally wrapped, along with the creature's spleen, in fresh ti leaves and laid them along side the body of the pig in the imu. With great reverence he covered over the corpse with more ti leaves. It was done. Now it was up to gods. They would accept him or not. He just had to wait.

Uncle had been watching Kiri perform the ceremony from the shade of the hut. When it was completed he passed Kiri the coconut shell containing the 'awa. Kiri raised it to his lips and felt the milky liquid slide down his throat, numbing his tongue on the way. Uncle filled the shell and drank from it himself. Then he filled it a third time and holding it aloft offered it's essence to the gods because it was well loved above all things by them. He lowered the shell and took a second draught before passing it on to Kiri who finished the bowl. Silently they squatted on the sand and waited. It was several hours before Uncle finally rose and instructed Kiri to open the imu. Kiri bent over the brown scorched leaves and carefully lifted them away and placed them to one side. His hands began to shake slightly as the sweet smell of cooked flesh assailed his nostrils. It was vitally important that he had packed the pit just right so that the fire would burn hot, but not too intensely, so as not to cook the pig too quickly and cause the flesh to fall away from the spine or the eyes to fall from their sockets. It had to be intact. It just had to be!

In slow motion Kiri rolled back the last leaves from the pig. He couldn't help it. A long sigh escaped his lips as he looked at the perfect sight of the animals back. It was intact!

He wanted to shout out, to dance around, to embrace Uncle. He wanted to run and tell someone, anyone that his pig had come from the imu intact, but his years of training silenced the emotions almost at once so that no one watching would have seen even a glimmer of excitement on his polished face.

Uncle looked long and hard at the pig and grunted, nodding his head. He showed no sign of emotion either, even though his old heart beat more strongly in his chest than usual and his throat was suddenly tight.

He looked deep into Kiri's eyes, then turned and walked off to the end of the beach where the mountains sloped down to sea. Kiri followed. Both men stood in the sand facing the impenetrable rock in front of them. Kiri knew that one further trial awaited him and that this also had to be performed to perfection.

"Kiri, it is now time," Uncle said. "Concentrate your prayers as you have been taught and you will succeed."

There was a moment's silence. Even the sound of the surf seemed to fade away. Kiri felt that time itself stood still and waited on him as he prepared himself for this final challenge. Uncle's voice rang out.

"Break the rock."

Kiri had worked most of his life to be in this position now. He felt no fear. He felt no doubt. Slowly and with great concentration he took his first deep breath. The fresh warm air raced in filling him completely. With deliberate slow intent he released the breath and the warm breeze caught it and carried it away. The next breath, impossible though it seemed, was even deeper than before and once again the breeze was there to take it from him. Closing his eyes he continued to breathe until he could no longer distinguish himself from the wind and his breathing fell into the rhythm of the pounding surf. The energy of the wind and the water poured into him. He felt his mana grow. He felt an intense tingling that excited the whole length of his spine. Soon his whole body vibrated with it and his head felt like it would split open. He closed his eyes and his sight was assaulted with blinding white light. He opened his heart to the gods and asked them to aid his task for he was nothing without them and, as he knew they would, they answered. Stretching out both arms towards the rock face, like a lightening bolt he released his mana and directed it at the rock in front of him. The side of the rock cracked like a dried gourd and fell in shards at his feet. At the same time something opened up wide inside him and even though he stood on the beach he had known for the last twenty six years, with a man that he had known all his life, he felt that from that moment on he was not the same person he had been and he wondered what path the gods had chosen for him.

Kiri and Uncle continued to live their lives together for another two cycles of the seasons, but as the time went on Kiri noticed that Uncle was becoming more frail. He performed less and less of the tasks allotted to them and spent more and more time at the water's edge communing with the sharks that were his family. Both he and Kiri knew that his time was near.

It was shortly after the onset of the winter storms that Kiri rose one morning to find that Uncle was still resting quietly in his bed instead of preparing the poi as was his normal custom. Kiri moved closer to the old man and knelt beside him. His eyes were heavy lidded and his breathing laboured. A low rattle escaped his mouth with each breath. Rising to his feet Kiri walked purposefully from the hut. He made his way inland to the rich source of ti plants that grew at the base of the falls. The plants were particularly lush here as the constant spray from the water kept them permanently misted and the leaves exuded vitality. He selected several of the best leaves to bring home. Dipping the gourd that he carried into the crystal water he filled it to the top. Tracing his footsteps back to Uncle his heart was heavy. He would perform the healing ritual on him of course, but in his heart he knew that the old man's time had come and he had to let him go. Before he returned to the hut, he went to the edge of the small headland that jutted out from the bay in an arc forming a small lagoon that kept that end of the beach at least a little protected from the winter swells. He placed his small burden carefully on a rock and stood at the very tip of the promontory.

Gathering his thoughts he began the familiar breathing pattern to raise his mana. When he was quite ready he raised his hands to the sky and let out the first of a long chant. The wind and spray began to whip at his body and his hair blew incessantly across his face and into his mouth. But nothing could deter him from the ritual that he now performed. The ancestors, too, had known that the last few days were Uncle's last, and very soon into the chant the familiar fins broke the water. Faster and faster they began to cut through the water, churning up the already boiling sea. As the last note of the chant was sounded, to be grabbed and carried away by the wind, they sank as one and Kiri was left looking at an empty sea.

Uncle was still asleep when he returned. Reverently, Kiri washed the old man's face and drizzled a little water from the gourd through his parched lips. It ran in small rivulets out of the side of his mouth. Taking the best of the ti leaves Kiri wafted it over the old man's head, flicking out to either side as if clearing smoke from a fire. Then he drew the leaf down each arm several times to brush away the stagnant energy. He repeated the process down Uncle's trunk and legs, then took hold of the old man's feet. There was always a slight chance that as the soul had not yet left the body he could push it back in from the soles of the feet. He took hold of Uncle's big toes and concentrated his mana. But the ancestors had summoned the old man and were waiting for him. The gods would not permit him to linger longer. As Kiri silently held the old man's feet he was aroused from his concentration.

"Kiri."

At first he thought he had imagined it. The voice was clear and strong. He looked up.

"Kiri," Uncle said again, his eyes wide open and looking straight at him.

Kiri left his feet and moved to the old man's side. Uncle's eyes never left him. Slowly, Uncle raised a clenched fist and held it out to him. Kiri placed his hand underneath the gnarled fist and felt the warm stone drop into his hand. Uncle opened his hand wide and clasped Kiri's hand. The stone sandwiched between the two. Uncle held his hand in a death grip, his eyes boring into him. Kiri felt the stone digging into the flesh of his hand and his arm grow suddenly numb. An ache began to spread from his fingers and make its way up his arm. As the ache progressed it grew in intensity until it became an intense pain that surged through his limb and finally exploded in his chest. The old man was passing on his final and most precious gift. His Mana!

Kiri's eyes began to fill with tears from the pain and from the grief of this parting. Uncle released his grip and his eyes, suddenly cloudy and unseeing, began to close. Kiri bent over him and touched his forehead and nose to the old man's in a final greeting of farewell. In a brief rush of breath Uncle released the last of his life force into the nostrils of his pupil and was gone.

Kiri opened his hand and stared at the dark green stone in his hand. He fought with every fibre of his being to control his anguish. As a Kahuna he had learnt to have mastery over his emotions but the pain of his loss and the transfer of mana had temporarily weakened him. Throwing back his head he opened his throat and let the full force of his grief escape in a frightening wail. There was just the one. Dropping the stone he walked outside.

Numbed by what had just transpired he walked in a trance to the water edge. The water lapped at his feet like a faithful dog. He turned his gaze to the rock face where it seemed such a short time ago he had had to prove himself to Uncle, prove he was worthy of carrying on the traditions. The rocks at the base of the cliff were polished smooth by the ocean. He felt their hardness against the soles of his feet in stark contrast to the yielding sand. Finally he approached the rock face and leaned his body against it, letting it support him. He focused on the mana of the rock and let it give him succour.

The rocks were the most ancient of all the old ones. They had existed since the world was formed and their permanence steadied him. He would have stayed there forever but the shout of a sea bird circling high above him roused him and he turned to walk back to the hut. Suddenly his feet went from under him. The support of the solid rock, which had felt so permanent a moment before, was no longer there and he felt the force of the rock jarring through his body as he landed forcefully on his back. A flash of lightening lit up his brain as the side of his head made contact with the stone. Then all was black.

It was dusk when he regained consciousness. The sun had slipped below the water line but was not yet sunk deep enough into the ocean so as to obscure it's light. Deep gold and red streaks stained the sky. When he tried to move, his head pounded like the surf on the rocks and his face and neck were stiff with blood. He staggered towards the surf, now quieter with the setting of the sun, and walked into the waves. When he was chest high in the water he sank his head beneath the waves and felt the caresses of the warm water on his wounds. Rising to the surface again he cupped his hands and gingerly began to wash the blood from his face. Searing pain darted through his skull each time he touched his head and several times he lost his footing, not finding the strength to resist the pull of the water. Gradually he grew accustomed to the pain, sinking it deep within, as he had done so many times before when he had taken the pain from a woman in child birth so that her work might be less. He rubbed more vigorously at the wound to encourage fresh blood to flow and cleanse the wound along with the salt water. Dipping down beneath the waves again he opened his eyes and watched with curiosity as the tiny rivers of bloods swirled around him. He wondered at the symbolism of the sun's blood painted across the darkening sky and his own blood staining the waters in front of him. Perhaps the sun knew something of his grief. Suddenly, his body stiffened with the shock of a new pain that seared into the flesh at the back of his leg, causing his body to arc backwards and water to rush into his lungs as a silent scream escaped his lips. It took only a second before he realised what had happened. He had not been vigilant. He had been too absorbed in his own grief. How could he have been so stupid! He felt the current of water created by the shark's wake rock his footing as it sped past him. Scrambling to find his feet again he felt the sandy bottom and pushed with all his might. His head cleared the surface and he spun around in a clumsy circle coughing and choking as he tried to clear his breathing.

They circled him slowly, each one close to the surface. He could gaze into each steely eye as they passed by. Fear gave way to resignation as he fought the urge to run for the shore and decided to stand still and wait. Death at least would be swift and he would see Uncle again sooner than he had imagined. In an eternity of time man and sharks watched each other, the slow circling becoming more and more mesmeric. Then, in an eye's blink, a dark body broke rank and dove towards him at great speed. Kiri closed his eyes and asked that the gods might receive him and grant him a quick exit from this life. The length of the shark's rough body grazed his as it brushed by. When he opened his eyes they had gone. Kiri ran for the shore as fast as his damaged leg would allow him, fear and relief spurring him on, momentarily anaesthetising the pain.

Dragging his useless leg up the beach to the hut, he packed the wound with herbs and wrapped it in the remains of the ti leaves that he had gathered earlier. He tied it as tight as he dared to stanch the bleeding. Uncle's body lay undisturbed in the room but Kiri knew that he could not leave it there for long. He had one last task to perform for the old man and no amount of pain could prevent him. Picking up the body, now strangely light and small, he wrapped it in tapa cloth. Dragging his injured limb, he slowly, with heavy heart and heaving breath, carried Uncle to the promontory he had visited earlier. With a short prayer to the gods, he summoned strength from he knew not where, to enable him to hoist the body of Uncle above his head and offer it to the gods. Shaking with a heavy mix of emotion and exhaustion, he finally tossed the limp body into the ocean and returned Uncle to his ancestors. Turning, he returned home and sank into a deep and fitful sleep.

The following morning his body ached in every part and a deep weariness encased him like a shroud. He forced himself to put some of the thick taro paste into a coconut shell and added some of the fresh water from the falls to make some fresh poi. He knew it would take several days before he would regain even a portion of his strength. When the shell was empty, he took some 'awa root and began to pound it to a paste with a stone. When it was done he added the remains of the water from the gourd to make a drink. He drank it down in one long swallow and sought comfort in the familiar numb feeling in his mouth. Soon he knew he would feel sleepy and he crossed the hut to lie down, but not before he had loosened the dressing on his leg and replaced the outer leaves with fresh ones. The ones closest to the wound, he left. He did not want to disturb the coagulated blood forming there. Using the power of his mind, he withdrew the excess energy from his leg. He knew this would slow down the flow of blood and reduce excessive loss through the damaged tissue. Once the wound had crusted and begun to knit, then he could increase the flow again to revitalize the area. In his mind's eye he saw the flesh knitting together and the skin returning to its normal texture. From the corner of the hut he carefully broke free the strands of a spider's web. With apologies to its maker, and after muttering a few words, he laid it across his bandaged leg calling on the weaving power of the spider to aid the tissue re-growth and seal the wound.

He slept through until the sun was high the following day. When he awoke his head was not quite so sore; but his leg pulled him up short as he tested it with a little of his weight as he tried to cross the room. Unwrapping the ti leaves he hopped down to the water's edge and allowed the salt water to cleanse the wound. Hopping back to the hut he managed to turn his leg slightly to get a look at the bite. Two large hemispheres of raw flesh encircled his calf muscle, black with congealed blood. If the jaws of the shark had snapped shut, as he knew they could have quite easily, he would have no muscle at all and walking would have been forever impossible. As it was, he realized as he gazed intently at the wound that he would be permanently marked with the sign of Uncle's 'aumakua.

Several days later, whilst walking at the edge of water to accustom his leg to weight bearing, Kiri came upon the thigh bone of a man washed up on the beach by the peninsula. The 'aumakua had returned that part at least of Uncle to him. He fell to his knees in thanks and red hot tears added more salt to the wound now encrusted on his face.

Time hung heavy around Kiri after Uncle's death. It cloaked him in a sombre cloud of despondency that he found impossible to shrug off. It took all his strength to continue with his duties, which now that there was only him, would sometimes keep him on the move for much of the day at times. Some days his leg, which had healed well, would ache right down to the bone with a gnawing reminder of his loss. If the healings that he was called to attend were likely to prove difficult, he took along the now dry thigh bone of Uncle's and the feel of it in his hand as he knelt to administer to the ailing would give him strength and focus for the job in hand.

Once again it was nearing the time of the festival to the god Lono to give thanks for the crops and the fishing and for good fortune. Again Kiri watched from the periphery as the preparations for the feasts took place. There was a lightness about the people at this time for above all else the Hawaiians loved to eat and delighted in any excuse for a feast. Next to eating they loved to dance. Kiri, entranced, watched the graceful movements of the hula dance. The men's dances were powerful yet they never became brutish, whilst the women's bodies moved with the same fluid motion as the ocean. Their hips traced figures of eight, rolling like incoming surf, whilst their arms told the stories of their ancestors and of the land that they called home. Kiri noticed that his depression must be lifting a little because he caught himself smiling softly as he watched the women. There was the suggestion of tingling in his groin that he had not felt for some long time. As he stood transfixed he became aware of another sensation. A tightening in his chest and a feeling of cold stone in his solar plexus. He realised that which he had known before, but never felt so acutely, which was his isolation from others and his deep loneliness.

By the end of the day he had come to a decision and as the sun began to sink he made his way to the heiau where previously Uncle and he had prayed before certain ceremonies. On his way he plucked a lush ti leaf and as he walked he scanned the ground in front of him for a suitable stone. He was almost at the heiau before he found it. It was the size of his fist, soft grey in colour and pitted all over with small holes. It was studded throughout with tiny chips of green crystal that twinkled as he turned it over in his hand to become accustomed to the feel of it. He knew that it had come from deep within the earth, a gift from Madam Pele. He knew that it had once been liquid fire but now it felt cool and comforting to the touch. Energized by the power of the earth and fire, it was perfect for his task. As he entered the heiau he put the ti leaf down and cradled the stone in his hand. He raised his voice and called to the gods, especially Madam Pele and her sister Poliahu, to hear his prayer and to send him someone to end his loneliness. A companion with whom he could share his life and his knowledge, who would understand the ways of the Kahuna and be content to live the life of service to the gods above all else. As he spoke forth his prayer he let some of his mana flow into the stone and felt it grow energized in the palm of his hands. Then he carefully wrapped the stone inside the ti leaf, making a small green parcel of it, and placed it carefully on the high stone in the heiau. Then he left and walked a few yards to sit at the base of a nearby palm to await the sign that told him that his prayer had been heard.

He closed his eyes and steadied his breath. It came, he knew not when, for he had slipped into that realm where time loses its cohesiveness and can stretch to an eternity or fly by in a moment, but when it came, it roused him so he was immediately awake. Somewhere off to his left, where the sun slipped into the ocean at the end of the day, and not too far away from him came the low, melancholic cry of an owl. The god Kūkauakahi, it was said, was consecrated in the body of the owl and it was well known that owls had saved many from death by averting danger. It was a powerful sign indeed, but one that Kiri was at a loss to totally understand. It was not the answer that he had expected. The god Kūkauakahi had answered his prayer, but why?

A few days after Kiri's prayer had flown to the gods, a messenger came to him from a small colony of people on the North side of the Island. Their chief, a man called Nanaka, had fallen ill. They themselves had no kahuna lapa'au at that time and had sent for Kiri to come and try to save the man. He was not an important chief as chiefs go; nevertheless, Kiri hastily placed a few roots and herbs into a piece of tapa cloth and set out for the journey across the Island. It would take him two days as the route was not straight forward and he did not want to arrive tired and lacking in the strength necessary to save the man. The North coast was composed of steep volcanic rock slopes that ran straight into the sea. Deep gullies cut into the rock so that it looked like the land dipped its fat fingers into the ocean to cool. Every night the rain gods dropped their blessing onto the high mountain peaks in the centre of the Island and the warm water made its way down the gullies to return to the waters of the sea before the next night's gift. The steepness of the slopes and the gushing water made foot holds difficult. Some had even plunged to their deaths on these high cliff faces. Over time nature had clothed them in green. The green fingers were deceptively and dangerously beautiful. In this part of the Island there were few beaches such as the one that Kiri lived on. The cliffs were in such a hurry to greet the ocean that they plunged knuckle deep into the foam.

The place of the chief was a small colony that had tucked itself between two such knuckles, in a place where, unusually, the land widened a little and flattened out somewhat. Here the people grew no taro. They lived from the sea and what little they could trade inland for the fish that they caught. The inaccessibility of the place made them isolated, except, that was, from the seaward side. Kiri, however, did not possess a canoe and was therefore forced to make his way on foot. He made good time but the gods in their wisdom had decided that the chief was to join his ancestors and when Kiri entered the hut where the man lay, the stench of death was everywhere. An old, wizened woman sat at his head bathing his brow with water taken from a wooden vessel beside her. Like a lot of the older women, she was of considerable bulk and the effort of leaning over the man made her puff and blow like a whale. She did not look up as Kiri entered but in a matter of fact voice informed him that the chief had taken ill with the sickness some ten days prior. Kiri placed his hand on the top of the man's head.

He divined that the man had pain in his chest, weakness of the eye and disturbance in the ears.

"His mana too is weak. What have you given him?"

The woman continued mopping the chief's brow.

"He has taken no food these past five days but he has been

purged," she said. "He has drunk the water from the sea and yesterday his bowels opened five times."

"What was the colour?" Kiri asked.

"First green, like old leaves then black," she answered.

Kiri knew that there was nothing to be done save making the man as comfortable as they could and await his demise.

While they sat by Nanaka, Kiri watched the old woman who took no notice of him at all. Her breasts lay supported on her great stomach and around her neck was what looked like a fine braid of human hair on to which was strung a tiny, delicate skull. Kiri supposed that it was the skull of a bird it was so light. A small river of sweat was running down her chest to disappear in to the deep cleft between her ample breasts. From where he sat it looked to Kiri as if the source of the tiny stream was the skull itself, water pouring forth from its gaping mouth. Her long hair, still quite black despite her age was pulled back from her face and a waxy flower of the melia tree was tucked behind one ear. Kiri loved the way all the island women adorned themselves with these beautiful flowers, filling the air around them in soft clouds of heady perfume. The one the old woman wore had lost its pertness and the edges of the petals were beginning to wilt. She had been here some time.

Death hung around the hut and the already hot and humid air was made more foul because of it.

"What do they call you?" he eventually asked.

"They call me Manu," she wheezed.

"I am… "

"I know who you are," she interrupted. Kiri decided not to try to pursue any conversation with her.

After a while, as the light began to fade, and the flaming

tapers that had been lit around the hut cast dancing shadows across the dying man's face, a young woman appeared to refresh the bowl of sea water beside Manu. As she placed the vessel back on the floor she took one of the old woman's hands and placed it gently on the edge of the container. It was the first time that Kiri had noticed that Manu was blind. The realisation came and went swiftly, however, for he found himself inexplicably mesmerized by the young woman at her side. He could not see her face as her hair fell in soft, shiny curtains around it. It was long enough to cover her breasts but he could see them moving beneath her hair as she gracefully finished performing her task. He slipped into a light trance and tuned into the woman. He found that she was having a disturbing effect on him. She had strong mana. She exuded a quiet power that was evident even in the smallest of her movements. Like Manu, she was completely naked but for the crisp flower in her hair—its petals still as fresh and heady as she herself.

His eyes did not leave her as she rose to leave, and so entranced was he, that at the moment she rocked back on her heels in preparation for standing, he too found himself rising to his feet so that they rose as one. Once standing, she stood for a moment and held his gaze in her own dark eyes. She did not avert her gaze as other women did when in his presence. A Kahuna was held in a mixture of fear and awe, but—and he could have imagined this in the tricks that the shadows were playing with the light— she seemed to give the ghost of a smile. It was not so much that her mouth moved but her eyes, as they held his, conveyed the message of a smile.

She walked purposefully from the hut and although she had ample room to give him a wide berth, he felt her breast brush across his arm and a small finger of pleasure teased through his body. He could have sworn that there was static in the air the like of which he had experienced on many occasions just prior to a lightening strike.

140

He felt rooted to the spot. He was torn between his duty to stay with the chief until the end and the overwhelming desire to follow this woman. The conflict paralysed him. His attention snapped back into sharp focus at the sound of Manu's voice.

"He is gone," came the sound from below him and Manu rocked back on her heels and let out a great sigh. Despite her bulk she moved well.

There were many preparations for the disposal of the chief's body. There were chants to be sung and men to be found to carry the body wrapped in a sheet of tapa to the cavern deep in the canyon where the chiefs were laid to rest. And of course there was the period of mourning.

Kiri looked for the young woman that he had seen the previous night. He could not see her, so he decided to go to the hut of Manu and give her the remains of the herbs he had brought with him. With no Kahuna in the village, it obviously fell to her to tend to the sick and the women of the community. As he approached the old woman's hut he saw the young woman again. She was squatting by a small fire pounding some leaves with a small stone which she held in her right hand whilst the crushed leaves lay in the hollow of a small wooden bowl that she steadied with the other. He felt a vice-like grip on his chest and his breath started to come in small bursts. This was something beyond his experience. It was not the normal reaction he experienced in the company of a beautiful woman—for she was beautiful—he could see that now. He had a momentary thought to turn and leave but she looked up and saw him and he was committed to finish his errand.

"I have brought these for Manu," he said. "They must be used soon and would most likely spoil on my journey home."

She rose and took the leaves from his hands, bowing her

head slightly in thanks. Then she returned to her task as if she had not felt the charge between them.

"The chief is to be buried tomorrow and I shall return to my village," he said.

It was an obvious statement, but his mouth felt compelled to utter something. Again, she replied with a slight bow of her head. There was to be no conversation then, he thought. Perhaps she is in awe of me after all. He stood for a few awkward moments more, and then turned to go. He took a step and then spun around again.

"Tell me who you are," he almost ordered. He had not meant it to sound that way, but the rush to get the words out had given them a power not intended.

She kept her head down whilst she answered. He thought it reverent on her part. She, however, did not want him to see the eagerness in her face as he spoke to her, or the slight rush of blood it brought to her cheeks.

"I am T'hane," she answered, "grand daughter of Manu, she of the bird tribe."

In that instant Kiri felt the hairs on the back of his neck prickle and in a distant part of his mind he heard the cry of the owl as it came to him that night at the heiau. The blood began to pound in his ears and this time it was his turn to bow his head in order to hide his face for he dared not speak. Had Kūkauakahi answered his prayer so soon?

Back home again Kiri struggled to get the girl out of his mind, but her face would float into his vision every time he relaxed his thoughts. Even when he was helping deliver a child he would look into the face of the village woman and T'hane's face would appear instead. He felt like a fish struggling on the end of a line. The more he resisted T'hane's pull the more he became ensnared and felt the outcome was inevitable.

Sitting quietly by the ocean one early morning he asked his own 'aumakua for help. What was he to do? The woman was interfering with the work he was pledged to do and he needed their guidance. Shortly he noticed a large fin lazily circling the water in front of him. A lone shark. Every so often the creature would rise a little from the water, yet not break his circular routine. It was a curious behaviour and one that Kiri had not observed before. Round and round went the shark with the peculiar arcing of its body every so often. It looked like it had no intention of leaving.

"What are you doing Mano?" Kiri silently asked the shark. "What are you trying to tell me?"

The shark continued circling. Kiri's eyes became locked on to the creature and still it continued to rise from the water every so often so that its upper back glistened in the light. Kiri watched the sleek, black back rise and fall, rise and fall, rise and fall—then he saw it! The shark only rose when he was on that part of the circle farthest away from the shoreline, never as it came round and closer into the beach. He only rose therefore to expose his right side to Kiri. As he rose the next time Kiri strained his eyes to look closer. He thought he glimpsed something but the shark had sunk again and was beginning his next turn towards the beach. Kiri waited. This time as the shark rose he saw it. On the shark's back just in front of the dorsal fin was a definite white mark!

As he at last recognized the spirit of Uncle, the shark dived. Kiri felt the emotion rise in his chest at such a contact with the old man. That alone eased his sense of loneliness, and he smiled gently to himself as out of nowhere a soft gentle rain began to fall. He turned his face to the sky and accepted the rain on his face. Truly the gods had spoken. Turning his gaze once more to the ocean, he saw the shark again. Uncle was back! This was indeed curious! This time he did not circle but cruised the length of the beach. Then Kiri saw the great fin turn. At that moment he had to close his eyes. He had been staring at the water too long and his eyes were strained. He was beginning to see double.

When he opened them again he realized that it was not his eyes that were playing tricks with him. Uncle had been joined by another shark. Together, they cruised the water in front of him and then as one dived. The ancestors had spoken and the signs were clear. He was not to be alone. That day he prepared for the journey. He took a fine piece of tapa cloth from the hut. It was a payment to him from the family of young man that he healed from the bite of a shark in a similar fashion to the way that he had healed himself. He also took a particularly fine specimen of conch shell that he had found while walking as a young man on this very beach. Finally he took up the necklace of kukui nuts and placed it over his head. He was ready. Today he would set out to get his new apprentice!

He knew that it was going against tradition. The knowledge that he had was usually passed on with the members of the same family, but hadn't Uncle himself broken with tradition himself all those years ago when he had taken Kiri as his. But, he argued to himself, he had the mark of the gods, and he raised his hand to touch his forehead, to the place where the black mark he was born with joined with the dark scarring left as a reminder of his fall on the day of Uncle's death. It was this first mark that had set him apart from other boys. When they looked at him they saw the sign of Kānehekili, the thunder god. Kiri's black moods and violent temper in his youth frightened the other children away, for the anger of the thunder god was black indeed.

144

Everyone knew that you could see it on the face of the sky before the thunder spoke.

So he had been chosen, and as a Kahuna it was his right to take an apprentice. In all the village he had seen no one that the gods had earmarked. He also knew that it was unusual but not unique to take a female to train, and this female had an uncommon degree of mana that singled her out as special. And lastly, had not uncle himself blessed his decision?

He had to use every ounce of his training to control the heady mixture of emotion that flooded through him as he came before Manu who was sitting in the shade of a palm, dozing he thought. Her head jerked upward before he was even twenty paces from her and her cloudy eyes looked straight at him. Summoning all his dignity as a Kahuna, Kiri came before her.

"Manu," he said. "It is I, Kiri. I wish to speak with you."

Manu sat motionless. Behind her dull eyes her mind was racing. What was this man doing back here in their village? He had not been summoned and she knew from the soft thud on the sand at her feet as he approached that he had brought something with him. She also smelt a subtle yet undisguised smell. Underneath the sweet aroma of cocoa nut oil he had washed in recently was a strong hint of anxiety and thinly disguised sexual need.

She motioned him to speak.

"I come to ask you to release T'hane to me. I wish her for my apprentice. I have brought you this fine tapa cloth," and he laid the cloth in Manu's lap, "as well as this fine shell—it is the best I have seen."

Manu ran her hands over the tapa, feeling the quality of it. She took her time. Not because she was particularly interested in the cloth but because it gave her time to think. Next she ran

145

her hands over the shell and as she lifted it from her lap she felt the energy it held. This was his own shell. The one that he used to summon the presence of the gods to his ceremonies. This was the shell that he had lifted to his lips and blown his life's breath into. It was infused with his mana. Her hands began to shake. This was a very personal gift.

As she sat there she knew that there was really only one answer that she could give this man. She was old and whilst she relied on the help of her grand daughter, she knew that her time here was not long and that she would soon leave T'hane alone. Their community was small and T'hane had shown little interest in the few young men of the tribe. T'hane was spirited, and Manu feared that she would fade as the melia flowers without the attention of a strong man. She would be better off with a Kahuna to look after her. The girl was gifted. She would always be in demand for the help that she could give to the villagers in times of sickness or birth and death but she was not a trained Kahuna. Here was a chance for her to have real power and influence on her people. Besides the man who now stood before was a Kahuna of immense power trained in the art of 'anā'anā. This was a dangerous man and one not to cross.

She slowly gathered her considerable bulk to rise. Kiri was tempted to move forward to help her but he maintained his stance. He had to impress this woman with the power of his position. Manu sensed the slight movement in him and nodded to herself. There was some kindness there at least.

Once standing she took a step toward him and stretching out her arms ran her fingers over his face. She began at the top of his head. Kiri drew back. It was kapu to touch the head of another unless you were a Kahuna, trained in the divination of sickness. But he put it down to her blindness and her fingers barely touched there before running down to his forehead. They lingered on the mark of the thunder god and he thought he felt them shake a little more. Then they moved to the scar left by the rock on the death of Uncle.

"Yes," Manu thought. "This man has great passion."

She moved swiftly over his chest and slid her hands to the tightness of his abdomen. Unexpectedly, she deftly slid her hand beneath the tapa cloth that he wore at his waist and with a firm and expert touch evaluated what else this young man might have to offer her grand daughter. Kiri flinched, taken totally by surprise. He had never been touched there by anyone before. His vow of celibacy had marked that place out for his own hand only. Manu registered his surprise and let out a low rumbling chuckle that rose to full blown guffaws that shook her entire immense body. She threw back her head, displaying her fine white teeth and the little skull jiggled violently at her breast as she gave vent to her mirth. Whist this was happening she did not release her hold on Kiri and he felt his manhood being shaken and jiggled as the woman fought to control her laughter. This was the most embarrassing and undignified position for him to be in. What was it with these two women? Did they have no fear of him!?

Manu got her mirth under control and much to Kiri's relief released her grip. The atmosphere grew suddenly strained as Manu, bending to run her hands down the inside of his thighs, touched the edge of the scar which began just below his knee and extended almost to the ankle.

"Mano," she whispered with a sharp intake of breath, instantly recognizing the mark of the shark.

She rose to stand before him again. What she saw behind her eyes was a young man of some considerable physical strength, who had strong features and immense mana. Who had been blessed, or was it cursed, by the gods not once but twice. He was both dangerous and naive. Her grand daughter would not have an easy time with him but, she mused,

147

thinking briefly of her younger days, T'hane would be well pleased with what he had to offer between his legs and it would be fun schooling him in those arts of which he had, by design, no knowledge of.

Even though she had no choice and felt that she had to acquiesce to Kiri's request, she decided to keep him waiting before giving her answer and told him that she would ask her 'aumakua for his decision, and rightly so, for it was their choice after all. That night, seated by the warmth of the fire she sat quietly in prayer. Eventually, from a small tapa cloth she took five smooth, black stones in her hands. In a clear voice she asked the pueo, her 'aumakua if it was permissible to allow her grand daughter to go to Kiri and then after shaking the stones in her cupped hands she threw them to the ground in front of her. Running her fingers over the configuration of the stones she got her answer, but just to make sure, her 'aumakua came to her. Swooping silently over her, Manu felt the movement of air from its gliding wings before she heard its plaintive cry. The owl had spoken. He would watch over T'hane.

There was little conversation between Kiri and T'hane as they made the journey back to his village but the air crackled between them. Both were subdued, neither one knowing what the outcome of this arrangement might be. Once back home Kiri set to work to construct a hut for T'hane. He might have defied convention by taking a female apprentice but he was careful not to anger the gods, or indeed the villagers, any more than was necessary by taking her into his own hut. It was kapu for men and women to share living space and even to eat together and he decided to abide by this ruling at least. The hut, when he was finished, was small and crude but sufficient. Like his own, it was built in the lee of the large boulders that came down the sea at the end of the beach. The rocks afforded some protection from the heavy squalls that blew in from the ocean but still remained close enough to the water so that, that night, the rhythmic lapping of the water lulled both of them to sleep after the efforts of the day.

The next morning when Kiri rose he saw that T'hane had beaten him into the water, and he could see her head bobbing on the surface of the waves as she swam to ease the discomfort of the journey from her aching limbs. Striding down to the water's edge, Kiri dove into the waves. He swam powerfully out from the shore without even glancing at the woman. After a few minutes he stopped swimming. He knew it was dangerous to go too far from the beach, for whilst it looked deceptively inviting from the shore line, with the sun glistening on the surface and the breeze just sufficient to create small white crests of spray, he knew that the waters were treacherous and had to be treated with the utmost respect at all times, even for one such as he who had been adopted by the shark family. He stood upright in the deep water and moved his legs, walking in the water, using just enough effort to keep himself afloat and no more. At this point he at last glanced over to where he had noticed T'hane when he first entered the water. She was nowhere to be seen. He caught a momentary flash of panic in his chest and then immediately scolded himself. She had probably gone back to the hut. Then another panic took him in it's grip. As he moved slowly in the water he felt something brushing past his leg. The memory of his encounter with the shark flashed into his mind. Instinctively he lashed out with his feet, but common sense told him that he had no chance of defending himself or of out swimming a shark. The mixture of panic and resignation held him in place. Then immediately in front of him, the waters broke and T'hane's grinning face appeared level with his own.

"Did I frighten you?" she smiled.

149

Kiri opened his mouth to chastise her but decided against speaking all together and remained silent. He did not want to give anything away to this woman.

Giggling loudly, in tones reminiscent of her grandmother, T'hane disappeared below the water again. Looking down through the clear water, Kiri could see her sleek body circling him. Her movements were easy and accomplished. Her long black hair streamed across her back as she powered her way through the water. After rising briefly to take another breath she sank below the surface again and Kiri saw her swim away from him a short distance. Then she turned and began to swim straight for him. Like a shark targeting its victim, she swam straight and true right at him. He expected her to rise up in front of him again and laugh in his face. But, as she got closer, he realized that she had no intention of surfacing and at the last moment he spread his legs to prevent her from crashing into them. She glided between them, her body brushing the inside of his thighs. He spun in the water to see her surface again, a wide grin on her face. Then she dived again. This time he knew what to expect when she powered towards him. But as she slipped between his legs this time, he was sure that she slowed her speed so that her body made contact with his for a fraction longer this time. Fire spread from his loins and warmed the pit of his abdomen.

The game continued for a few minutes more, with Kiri's pulse racing more each time she made a pass. The next time she came towards him he vowed to reach out and catch her. T'hane dived again and moved towards him. Kiri felt the blood building in his head, felt the longing in his chest and the need in his loins. He wanted her so badly it was beginning to hurt. He held his breath, pacing himself to get the timing just right. She was a few feet in front of him. His body went tight with anticipation, then, with perfect timing of her own, T'hane swerved to pass him on his left her hand trailing behind her to brush his sex before she made swiftly for the shore line!

150

Kiri stayed in the water a while longer waiting for his mind and his genitals to calm down. When he did finally walk up the beach to his hut to eat, T'hane was gone.

Over the next few days they kept an uneasy distance. When Kiri looked over to where T'hane was working at picking herbs or grinding them into pastes as her grandmother had taught her, or tending the fire, she would lower her head and her face would remain hidden in the sleek folds of her hair. Kiri was confused. Does she desire me? he thought. The idea that he might be attractive to a woman was one that had not occurred to him before. He dismissed it out of hand. She is just missing the attentions of men, he decided. She is just playing. She can not seriously want to join with me.

From behind the safely of her hair, T'hane was smiling impishly to herself. Nothing could have been further from the truth. She wanted this man but she had no intension of just giving herself to him. She wanted to play with him awhile first. She wanted to build the obvious passion between them so that he would want no other and be firmly and forever hers. She felt that the gods had put them together, but that did not prevent her from manipulating the pact to her advantage. As a young girl, growing up in her village, sex and play intermingled at every opportunity and she had been well schooled in the ways of pleasure by her grandmother. She knew that in a society where sex was both a pleasurable and acceptable way of passing the time for everyone, you had to employ certain wiles in order to keep a man from straying. For the last few years she had spurned the advances of the men in the village. They all wanted too much from her and were not as skilful in pleasuring her as she them. She had decided to remain alone. But the passion still burned in her and she was beginning to find it hard to resist the temptation now before her.

The first birthing that Kiri had to attend after T'hane's arrival promised to be difficult, so he took her along with him. He had been summoned by the woman's sister. The child had struggled to arrive for a whole day and a night and when Kiri arrived it was clear that the baby was not in the correct position for birth. Running his hands over her abdomen he could sense that the child was coming into this world the wrong way. He was pleased to see that T'hane had an easy way with the woman that immediately put her at her ease. She had skill in her hands also, as she massaged the woman's belly and sang to her to ease the pain. Kiri coated his hand in coconut oil and eased it into the woman. Moving slowly and with his other hand moulding and pressing on the abdomen he tried to turn the baby. He soon realized, however, that the labour had progressed too far and that if this child was to born at all it would be with its feet first. As the woman struggled with the increased pain, Kiri began once again to increase his mana. Instructing the woman to look into his eyes he began to take her pain into his own body.

T'hane watched enthralled as the woman's breathing slowed and a slight smile spread across her face. She saw her body soften and open as the pain subsided. She realised that the child had a better chance to come safely into the world if this mother was relaxed. Glancing at Kiri's face she saw his brow knit in pain for a moment and then he, too, relaxed.

With the woman no longer fighting the pain, Kiri was able to ease the legs and pelvis of the boy child into the world. Oiling his hand again he eased his fingers past the child's body and into the woman to manipulate the shoulders through the birth canal. Finally, the head followed and the child came free with a flood of bloody liquid. Kiri sat back on his heels and let out a deep sigh. The small body was cradled in his hands momentarily before the mother reached out to claim her child and hold it to her breast. Both he and T'hane could not resist smiling. After a few moments, T'hane leaned forward to cut the cord and waited for the afterbirth to appear. When it had not appeared a few minutes later, it was she who reached inside the tapa bag to take out a few leaves which she instructed the woman to chew on whilst she continued to gently massage her stomach. A short time later the afterbirth appeared. Kiri was pleased. She had done well. She obviously had skill already and might therefore be amenable to further instruction. As they were leaving, T'hane turned towards him.

"How did you do that?" she asked. "How did you take that woman's pain? Can you teach me how to do such a thing?"

"All in good time," Kiri responded. "All in good time."

He was tired. Taking someone's pain took considerable effort on his part and he didn't have the energy for instruction now. This was something that he would teach her later. For the moment it was important that he got on with the task of relaying to her the chants that were the basis of his art. She would have to practice them until she was hoarse, until they slipped from her tongue like water infused with the energy of the heart. That would be her first task. He began by instructing her in the study of the Kumulipo. This ancient chant described the beginning of time and how the earth came into being. It told of how the seas and lands were created from the original great beings, now deified as gods, and described the lineage of the peoples. He taught her also the kaona, the hidden meanings which lay beneath the surface of the words that she spoke.

Over the next weeks T'hane struggled with the complex task of learning by heart the chants that Kiri taught her. She would take herself off, far away from the beach, and further inland, away from the ears of her teacher, and there in a grove of palms would practice until her voice or her patience gave out. Since the game in the surf that day there had been no

153

opportunity to tease Kiri. She still knew that he burned for her with a passion that was palpable yet he had made no move. They had fallen into the role of master and disciple, with him, sometimes harshly, passing on skills to her, or listening to her chant with a dark scowl on his face. She was convinced that she was making a complete mess of everything and prayed vehemently to the gods for their forgiveness of her feeble efforts. She had the feeling that the gods were more forgiving than Kiri seemed to be. He gave her no praise or encouragement at all. After each evening of listening while she made her way through a long sequence of chants, he would always rise to go to bed with the words:

"Practice more."

For his part Kiri knew that if this woman was to succeed in the task ahead of her he had to be strict with her as Uncle had been with him. When she came to use these gifts there would be no room for mistakes. Her life and the lives of others would depend on her knowing, with absolute certainty, what she was doing. He, above all, knew how arduous a task it was, especially to a young woman full of fun and passion. His own lustful cravings he kept in tight check, although it was proving more and more difficult by the day.

Over the months the serious business of teaching took over their lives. T'hane's accomplishment of the chants was progressing well and she picked up the healing skills as if born to it, which indeed he felt she had been. She had already received many years of expert tuition from Manu. One aspect of the healing work that Kiri had to teach her, however, was very different from anything that her Grandmother had schooled her in. Kiri had spoken to her many times about the necessity to change the energy pattern of the physical body in some circumstances. For many illnesses the use of medical herbs and massage were enough to regain health but sometimes, if the illness was particularly grave, or if bones were broken, it became necessary to work at a very deep level to change the very matrix of the body in order to effect healing. Sometimes when a person was close to death, the working of the energy body in a particular way could reverse the process and the person's mana could be coerced into remaining within the physical realm for a while longer, should this be the wish of their 'aumakua. It was also work that benefited the dying. Kiri, like all Kahunas, recognized that sometimes there was nothing he could do for the dying other than to ease their passage to Po, into the darkness of eternal life, and speed their return to the ancestors.

All these things he told T'hane. He told her of the puka, the places on the physical body that allowed for communication with the realm of the 'aumakua. How it was important that these puka were open so that the 'aumakua could intervene in the healing process, so that the gods might succeed where man had failed. He instructed her carefully in the state of mind it was necessary to enter into whilst performing this task and the exact hand placements.

What T'hane had not been ready for, or could even have imagined beforehand, was the incredible connection that she encountered whilst practising this work on Kiri. Each time there came a point in the procedure when their very souls seemed to join as one. She was gripped in an escalating spiral of joy and expansion that was pure bliss. Floating in this timeless state, the return to earth was always a disappointment.

When he believed she was ready, he took her along to the next healing on a dying man that needed just such intervention. T'hane followed everything that Kiri had told her. Whilst Kiri held the feet of the unfortunate man, she went to his head and laid her hands gently on his shoulders. She looked briefly at Kiri before closing her eyes and entering the deep trance state that she had been practicing. Of course, working like this on a sick person was quite unlike the practice sessions that she had done with Kiri. She had come to know his energy so well that she did not encountered any surprises while working. In this instance as she moved from the man's shoulders to place her hands on his pelvis and liver, and begin the process of dissolving into the physical body to gain access to his mana and open up the puka, she found herself blocked. Try as she might, there seemed no way that she could do what was needed. After a moment she heard Kiri's voice softly in her ear and felt his hands resting lightly on her shoulders.

"Do not try so hard. Be patient, little one. Just sink deep into yourself and wait—but keep your intention clear."

T'hane felt the tension go out of her body. She hadn't even been aware that she was tightening up until Kiri pointed it out to her through his contact. She also released the grip from her mind, and soon she was gone. Her body seemed to have dissolved and she was awash with waves of pure sensation; then she became aware of a deep connection to the dying man. The connection became stronger and she became aware of the spiral of sensation that seemed to climb higher and higher through infinite space. It was accompanied by the feeling of pure joy as their two souls locked together. It reminded her of the sensations that she had experienced often with Kiri. Gradually she felt herself returning and she opened her eyes slowly to look at the man. Kiri, the man and she were surrounded in a thick golden fog. It was so quiet that she could hear the silence pressing in on her. Everything was filled with such beauty.

As Kiri and she left the man a little while later, the quiet contented silence between them remained along with the strong connection. Eventually T'hane spoke.

"What I experienced back there," she said, speaking slowly and deliberately, "was just as I experience with you. I

156

had not thought to ever experience anything like that with another, especially a man I know not, and a man who has none of the mana of you."

Kiri smiled.

"The soul of man is his greatest gift. There are those who use it and those who hide it away, sometimes even forgetting where they left it. Did you think that your soul would not be ecstatic, to join with the soul of another, free from the bonds of the body and the mind? Did you not feel the joy of that communion? All beings are thus underneath."

Kiri looked at T'hane and saw the impact of his words register in her face.

Suddenly he laughed out loud. "Ah, the power of real love," he said and quickened his step for home.

As the time that they spent together lengthened, a mutual respect developed between the two of them, but T'hane always felt that Kiri's usual gruffness with her was his way of preventing the relationship from spilling over into other areas of interaction that were normal for a man and woman. Even so she longed for him to relax his guard just a little so that she could get emotionally closer to him. Whilst employed with the work, concentration on the task was complete and often they worked as one unit, building their joint mana to great limits that taxed their bodies and minds as they sought to control the power they were capable of unleashing. Kiri had worked in this way with Uncle, but this was different. The heady combination of the sexual energy available to them as man and woman increased the mana far beyond that which Kiri and T'hane had ever experienced on their own. However, even as this sexual tension was brought to the task in hand, when the work was done they returned to the teacher and student role that kept them at a safe distance.

After breakfast one morning Kiri set out along the beach. T'hane watched him. He seemed to be scanning the shore line and every so often he would stop to crouch down and pick up something from the sand. When he had walked almost the entire length of the beach he turned and set off into the trees. He wasn't gone long and when he returned he was carrying a small pile of oddments in his hands. He sat down by the hut and began to assemble something from the things he had found. T'hane watched him attentively. First he picked up a length of dried stick. On closer examination she noted that it was in fact a length of dry stem from the reed grasses that grew close to the shore line. Once dry it was quite hard and stiff. Kiri looked at the stick and then snapped it at one end. He picked up another and did likewise. In a short while he had a small pile of sticks in front of him of differing lengths. Picking up two of the sticks he began tying them across one another with a length of coconut fibre. He worked attentively. Sometimes he seemed unhappy with the length of stick that he had chosen and would break a little more off, sometimes several times until he was quite satisfied with the length. T'hane watched as gradually a shape began to take form. T'hane had no idea what Kiri was making but she knew enough not to interrupt him with questions. As he bent forward over his labours, Kiri took frequent sideways glances at T'hane through the curtain of his hair to check that she was paying attention. He was pleased to see that, like all women, her curiosity was keeping her sitting quietly and watching.

Eventually Kiri held up what he had been working on. In some ways it resembled a badly composed spider's web. The sticks were tied together in a fashion that created a web effect but without the precision of the spider's art. Where the sticks crossed over one another, Kiri then secured a small shell from the collection at his feet that he had picked up on the beach. This improved the look of the thing, but T'hane thought it a poor work of art; not that it was badly made but that it looked misshapen and unbalanced. Kiri held the piece up to the sky in front of him, inspecting it intently. He seemed satisfied and then, turning, held it out to T'hane. T'hane held out her hands to receive the gift. She bowed her head in acknowledgement. She was unwilling to speak, not quite knowing what to say. Kiri got to his feet.

"Let me know when you have discovered its use," he said and walked away.

T'hane held up the object in front of her. She had no idea of what it could possibly be any good for. It was too small to carry anything in, and besides the gaps between some of the sticks were quite wide and uneven. The fibre that bound the whole thing together was so soft and the whole thing bent so easily that she surmised that any weight on it would cause it to buckle out of all recognition. She assumed that Kiri probably hadn't just made it badly and that carrying objects was therefore definitely not one of its uses. She ran her fingers over the surface of the smooth sticks, her finger tips bumping over the shells at intervals. She wondered if she could pick up a clue through her fingers that her eyes were missing. None came to her. In frustration she carried it to her hut and set it aside. Maybe it would come to her later.

Sometimes Kiri would allow T'hane to massage his leg when the wound from the shark played him up, mostly when he had walked all day or been forced to squat for hours. Her hands were soft and pliable and felt like silk on his skin. She would begin by sitting with his foot in her lap as he lay stretched out face down in the sand with the sun at his back. Oiling her hands with coconut oil she would begin to work deep between his toes and between the tendons of his foot.

Her fingers sought out every tense spot and eased it away. She would pull gently on each toe joint and then pull off the end of each toe quickly to release the energy. Kiri could feel the tingle of the release travel up his body, snaking round his spine to burst like a bubble at the base of his skull. Moving over the instep of the foot her fingers untied the knots in the rest of his foot and around the heel. Then she would pick up the foot, and resting it on her shoulder, start to work his calf and around the scar tissue. Starting at the heel she would draw both her forearms down the side of his calf to the knee, and then squeezing her arms together apply pressure to the muscle as she drew them upward again towards his heel. Often as she started, the movement made Kiri wince as a dull ache followed in the wake of her touch, but as the muscle softened in response to the urgency of her touch he revelled in the spreading warmth and the easy flowing connection between his skin and hers.

Laying his foot down again, T'hane would work the softened calf muscle and the back of the thigh with long strokes of her forearms across the muscle fibres, bringing heat from the depths of his body until the muscles burned with inner fire. Then placing both her arms across the back of his knee she would slide them apart to encompass the entire length of his leg from the top of the thigh to his heel in long integrating strokes. The strokes became lighter and lighter and began to concentrate not so much on the tight muscle but the life force that she now knew so well. Each pass of her forearms mobilized his energy and he felt it flooding through him, wave after wave of sensation that floated his mind on a sea of tranquillity. His body lost its definition so that he felt his whole being moved with every stroke of her hands like a piece of seaweed caught on the current, ebbing and flowing in a sea of energy. Often she would leave him caught in the delight of the flow until the energy once again subsided.

When he came to again he was always alone on the sand.

160

He always felt empty afterwards. His body had reached out to connect with her and it revelled in the contact, fed on the contact, satiated itself in the contact, but was left wanting more and more each time. He had also noticed that as they worked together more and more both their minds became as one. Much of the work indeed was about training T'hane to do just that so that she could know not only the workings of his mind, but of others, so that she could reach inside them to root out the cause of their disease or to seek out the truth of a situation. The 'awa helped her to communicate with the gods but it was Kiri who helped her to communicate with the minds of others. Still more and more it was becoming apparent that they thought as one even when not engaged in the work. Often these days they would find themselves speaking together, not at odds with each other, but as one voice. The same thought would occur to both at the same time. This always made T'hane laugh and even Kiri had allowed himself a small grin on these occasions. More and more he felt himself bonding with this woman and he missed her presence when she was absent from him from time to time.

T'hane, too had noticed their growing link. Often she knew his thoughts or could anticipate his needs before he spoke them. She noticed that more and more, as they sometimes sat together quietly at the end of the day before going to their huts, that the silence between them spoke volumes and satisfied them without the need for words. In fact words would only spoil the moment. More and more she longed for that final act of union that they had denied each other. She realized as she thought about it that they had not even acknowledged the need that each had for the other. They had skirted round it, darting away from each other at each accidental encounter, only to be magnetised back again a short while after. But even so the force field that kept them apart also held them together and T'hane decided she could not wait much longer to act.

As always, however, the gods did not make it easy for her. The next few days were busy and at the end of a long bout of births and deaths when they were both about to fall on to their sleeping mats exhausted, a young man beat a path to Kiri.

Reverently he fell to his knees at Kiri's feet. He was clearly frightened and not just of Kiri.

"I come to beg for your help," he gasped. "I know of no other to turn to, you must come, you must come."

Kiri stooped down and took the young man by the elbow drawing him to his feet.

"Who are you to say that I must come?" He spat the words from between clenched teeth.

T'hane immediately sensed that something different was happening here, something that she had not experienced before. She had never seen Kiri act in this way. She felt his mana increase as soon as he touched the man's arm. She felt him reigning it back in through his clenched teeth.

"Forgive me, great Kahuna," bleated the man. "It is my father. Last evening as he sat at his meal he suddenly began to drool from the mouth and talk incoherently. Then last night as he slept a large blue-black mark appeared on his arm, and this morning he cannot rise from his bed. I fear if nothing is done soon he will die."

Kiri stood erect, staring straight ahead.

"What have you to offer?" he said eventually.

Kahuna's did not give their services for free. They lived off the donations given to them by those that sought their help. The more arduous the task, the greater the donation required.

"We are not a wealthy family," the man lied. "We have had a good crop of taro this year however and we can offer you some of that."

Kiri looked hard and long at the man. He should know better than to lie to a Kahuna he thought. Doesn't he know that his feeble mind is as clear as the forest pools to me.

"Not enough," he said harshly.

"Great Kahuna," said the man, bowing his head low, "we have little more that we can offer."

"You are asking me for the life of your father," Kiri stated icily. "You are asking me to perform magic of the highest kind. Magic that puts me in fear of my own life. There must be more. It is not sufficient!"

Kiri's black eyes bored into the man.

Realising that if he wanted Kiri's help he would have to strike a better deal, the man swallowed loudly and whispered, "There is a pig, not a large one, it is the last of our present litter. But it will grow—this I can offer."

The man looked as if he would vomit.

"Go home," responded Kiri in a tight voice, "go home and await me there."

The young man scuttled off across the beach, the tears that he had been holding back now streaming unrestrainedly down his face.

Kiri turned to his hut and went inside. T'hane followed him to the entrance. He picked up Uncle's thigh bone and brushed roughly past her.

"Wait here," he hissed.

"Wait, but why? Why can't I come with you?" T'hane

163

asked.

"Wait."

"You have never told me that I cannot accompany you before. What is happening? Why must I wait here?" T'hane continued, her voice tinged with a mixture of anger and concern.

"I do not have to answer to you, woman," Kiri snapped back.

T'hane ran round in front of him to stop him in his tracks. She looked deep into his face and drew back startled. The thunder god stared back at her. Kiri's face was black with anger. His eyes burned into her. She felt the force of his power and for the first time was very afraid. She stepped aside and he strode off across the sands. T'hane sat down heavily on the beach, deflated like the sails of the waka on a still day. She had never seen Kiri this way. What was it that had prompted such a violent reaction in him? She turned to watch his figure growing smaller and smaller as he hurried to the village. He had taken the thigh bone of Uncle so she realized that the work he was to perform required strong mana but other than that she knew nothing.

It was then that a thought started eating at the corners of her mind. All the time that she had been with Kiri she had always obeyed his every word. This she knew was required of her as his apprentice, but now it was not concern for the Kahuna that forced her to her feet but for the man that she sensed beneath the surface. The man that she had had all too brief encounters with, yet knew intimately. With growing resolve she came to her feet. If she stayed close to the trees at the edge of the beach, she surmised, she could track him without him realizing. If she closed her mind to him, he may not realize her intent and sense her presence. Movement is silent over soft sand, so that was no worry; and with her mind out of reach, Kiri had no idea of his pupil's reckless and disobedient behaviour. She tracked him to a large hut near the centre of the village surrounded by several others. She realized then what Kiri had already intuited, that this man's family was of some importance. Desperate that Kiri should not discover her, T'hane decided to stay tucked away at the back of a hut next to the one that Kiri now entered. Sitting with her back to it she took a few minutes to steady her breath, which she was sure could be heard by the entire village, and waited.

As Kiri entered the hut he realized that his concern was well founded. Immediately he dropped to one knee and holding the bone of Uncle before him began to chant the prayers. He called upon Uncle and he called upon the ancestors to aid him in this onerous task, and he prayed that they would protect him and bring him safely through the ordeal. Only when he had finished the long chants did he begin the slow breathing ritual to increase his personal mana. When he was ready, he asked the members of the family to leave. Who knew what could happen. He did not want them at risk. Besides if he was right, the fewer sources of life energy in the place the better.

He moved over to the man lying before him and placed his hand gingerly on his arm. Immediately his fears were realized. A powerful pull was being exerted on his hand even though he barely touched the man. In an instant his mind saw what his hand could only guess at. The thought form, for that was what it surely was, was awesome indeed. The bulk of its body, and therefore Kiri surmised, the point of entry, was in the man's right arm. Looking closely he noticed a freshly healed scar just above the elbow. Long and thin, but quite deep, it looked as if he had caught the edge of a spear which was probably aimed at his chest. Raising his arm he had managed to deflect the cutting edge but he had not escaped entirely. Someone didn't like the man and when the spear had failed other weapons had been brought into play. The black, dense body of the thing was not the only thing Kiri became aware of. It had numerous writhing tentacles like the he'e. Except this was no creature of the deep, and the sinewy tentacles were spread from the man's arm reaching deep into his chest and up into his throat. It was the strongest possession that he had yet encountered. He withdrew his hand quickly to his side. As his mind acknowledged its existence he felt its power in the energy field between them. He summoned his mana.

This time he placed both his hands firmly on the man's arm. Immediately he felt it strike out and ensnare his hands. He was trapped. The creature and he were locked together in a deadly embrace. He knew then that this was the work of a powerful Kahuna, well trained in the art of 'anā'anā. Sorcery of this magnitude he had not encountered before. He hoped that his power was greater than his adversary's. Right now he was locked in battle with the creature. Each time he took hold and began to pull it from the man's body he was met with equal force pulling his hands deeper inside. Each time he increased his mana and released it down his arms and into the creature he felt a surge of strength flowing back at him. It was feeding on his mana and growing stronger. He knew that if he relaxed his concentration for a minute the creature would gain the upper hand and begin drawing more of his mana and so increasing its strength until not only the host that it inhabited would die, but Kiri's life also would be threatened.

These thought forms were often sent by Kahunas who were paid well for the task, though Kiri knew of no other capable of this kind of work on the Island. Distance was not always a factor, however, and a good Kahuna trained in 'anā'anā could send a thought form over great distances, even from the other islands. They entered the body when the person was weak with illness or injury or distraught with emotion. Taking hold, like a blood sucker, they begin feeding

166

on the host energy, growing bigger and stronger in the process until the host finally died. Someone had wanted this man dead badly enough to hire the services of a powerful Kahuna indeed to perform the task.

Kiri continued to battle but it was with growing concern that he realized that his strength was waning. The creature had been in the man some time and was already strong from the man's not inconsiderable mana. It had also been able to draw from Kiri. Its growth was phenomenal. Kiri noticed his mind becoming cloudy and his eyes weak. His mind and his mana were the weapons he needed to fight this thing. He must hold on to them at all costs. He could not allow himself even the idea of failing however he knew his concentration was slipping.

Behind the hut T'hane suddenly became very concerned. A chill of fear was running down her back and settling in her bowels. Something was very wrong, very wrong indeed! Remembering her training she quelled the emotion and focused her mind. Slowly she began opening it again to Kiri. She shut it again with a start as a writhing black figure swam before her eyes. Black bile came up and caught in her throat.

"What was that!" she gasped.

At the same time she sensed that Kiri was loosing his mana at an alarming rate. Then out of nowhere she heard the cry of the pueo. Swooping low across the ground in front of her it glided up before her, passing within a foot of her face and alighted on the top the large hut. The bird's flight toward her awoke T'hane from her confusion. She suddenly knew what she had to do. She had done it before many times and this was no different she argued. Quickly she began to build her mana. She did it more rapidly than she was used to, but the situation called for great urgency. It didn't matter that she didn't know what was going on. Kiri needed her energy. He would know what to do with it.

Inside the hut, Kiri suddenly felt the tide turn. A new strength came into his body and his mind. Drawing deeply on it he took an enormous breath and was thankful for the extra surge of energy that accompanied it. He would have to be quick and act now. If he hesitated, even for a moment, then the creature would continue to draw on this new energy source and all would be lost. He had to take it by surprise. Summoning every ounce of his strength and focusing his mind intently, he heaved the writhing thought form free of the man. Losing strength rapidly as it separated from its host, Kiri strode outside with it and asked the ancestors of the rocks, which were the oldest of the old ones, to take the creature and contain it until it disintegrated. He plunged his arms into soft earth and felt the creature leave. Turning round to re-enter the hut he glimpsed her.

"T'hane!"

He should have suspected that his increase in power had been helped by her but it was still a surprise to see her.

"What are you doing here?" he bellowed, his face still set, but no longer glowering black with rage. "I had forbidden you to come and yet here you stand. What have you to say?"

T'hane looked at the ground at her feet. Her mind became blank and remained that way so that search as she may she could find no explanation that would be acceptable to the man in front of her. When her response did come it was as much a shock to her as to Kiri, who had not yet taken his eyes from her. A surge of emotion welled up inside her. It rushed head ward and spurted from her mouth before she could put the locks in place to hold it.

"I came, you fool, because I sensed real danger! I could see and feel the rage in you as you listened to that boy and I was afraid for you and if you can not see that what I did I did for you then maybe I should return to Grandmother and leave you to your stupid chants and potions."

Kiri, felt his anger swell. He who had spent his life trying to control his emotions was still not comfortable either with his own or T'hane's.

"And who gave you the job of looking after me?" he bellowed.

"Looking after you. Looking after you!"

T'hane was now so angry and upset that words became incoherent to her and she again struggled to come back with a response to his unkind words. Could he not be grateful? she asked herself. Could he not at least say thank you!

"I came here, against your wishes, against even my own concerns, to give what help I could to you in this situation. I didn't know what was happening, I only knew that maybe, just maybe, I could be of use to you, and yes, I admit to curiosity, but I came because above all… "

Here she stopped to quell the emotion that was choking her, catching at her throat making it difficult to speak. She took a deep breath in and controlling the out breath let the words ride on it in an orderly manner.

"I came because I have real concern for your welfare. You are important to me. Not because of what you can do, powerful as that is, but because of who you are."

She paused again. The very air held its breath in the silence that followed.

"I have found in myself, over the time I have been with you, a great love that I did not believe possible. My actions tonight were at love's command, not mine, and certainly not yours."

The old defiant look came across her face and she looked

hard into Kiri's face which was motionless. In fact he seemed to be holding his entire body in a state of readiness, for what neither he nor T'hane knew.

Suddenly he could contain himself no more and without speaking turned and made his way home, which was where T'hane found him a short time later on her return.

She did not speak to him again and he did not make any effort to speak to her. That night as they lay in their huts each one wrestled with the impact of T'hane's words. They had rung true in the silent air. She had spoken her love aloud and it could not be taken back. That which had been unacknowledged for so long was now confronting them both like an angry boar. There was no place to run and hide, it could not be ignored or distracted. The only course available was to kill it immediately or embrace the danger and the potency of the moment and accept the challenge of it no matter what the outcome. T'hane knew in her heart that the only course open to her was to accept her feelings and try her best to get this stubborn man to admit her into his heart. In his hut Kiri lay sweating with a cocktail of fear and excitement, frantically thinking of ways to drown this new emotion at birth.

T'hane and Kiri found it uncomfortable to be around each other for the next couple of days. Neither knew how to broach the subject and so decided to ignore it, and each other, as that made life at least tolerable if not easy. Kiri, switched even more strongly into teaching, laying down the boundaries of their relationship even more strongly. T'hane felt them more keenly each day and she grew more saddened as the time passed and Kiri made no move toward her.

"Have you discovered the use of the object yet?" he growled at her one day.

"Not yet," she replied dropping her head in shame.

To be honest she had not looked at the weave of sticks since the day Kiri had given it to her. It still lay in her hut where she had left it that day. She had thought about it of course but the more she wrestled with it's possible meaning the more frustrated and angry she became.

"Why can he not just tell me," she spoke aloud under her breath. "He's supposed to be the teacher after all."

She could not believe how heavy her heart weighed in her chest. It took all her will to perform the tasks she was set and to do them with good grace. To do otherwise would have been an insult to the gods. However as time went on she cared less and less about dishonouring the 'aumakua. If they loved her as she had been taught, how could they not intervene for her and turn this man's heart?

She was surprised after a while when Kiri asked her to once again work his leg. It benefited from her touch and he was tired of putting up with the ache. He had often wondered why it was that he could not blot out the discomfort from this wound when he was capable of taking great pain into himself and then dissolving it so that it no longer affected him. When he asked the 'aumakua he received the puzzling reply that it was their way of ensuring his attention—as if he could forget them! But he had noticed that when he was a little lax in his work or unaware of an impeding situation because he had not noticed the signs, the ache in his leg would increase. It had been increasing for a while now and he wasn't sure what he was missing.

Stretching his naked body out on the warm sand, he lowered his foot into T'hane's hands positioned on her lap as he had done so many times before. The sun warmed his back and he was grateful for it. There was nothing, he decided, quite so good as the sun on your back. With a sigh, he relaxed a little deeper into the sand and waited for T'hane to work her magic on his leg. She began working in between his toes as usual, stretching out each tendon and then easing the tension from the foot by twisting on it, first one way then the other. The glow from his foot competed with the warmth of the sun and Kiri felt content. It had been a strain keeping his distance from T'hane and maintaining an air of authority. He found it hard to sustain on many occasions. He just wanted to give in and rest and ease the bothersome deep ache from his leg. T'hane's forearms squeezed down the calf muscle and then pulled back up again and for the first time Kiri became aware of her breasts brushing against the outside of his leg with each rhythmic movement up and down his leg. She had obviously placed his foot over her shoulder as usual but somehow her position had shifted slightly and his lower leg now nestled at her breast. Perhaps she had always done it this way Kiri thought, perhaps the gods are right I don't always notice everything. Who can notice everything?

T'hane eased his leg down on to the sand and began to work across the back of his calf and thigh. Once again the tissue began to burn under her touch. Then he felt her place her arms across the back of his knee to begin the long strokes outward to his heel and to the top of his thigh. This was the most delicious part to him and he settled into himself to enjoy the waves of energy that she released. Lulled by the sweetness of the sensation, he was surprised but not alarmed to feel T'hane extending the sweep of her forearms so that the stroke, instead of stopping at his thigh, swept on and up over the mound of his buttock, snaking round the base of his spine before retreating like the waters of the oceans back down to his knee. Stroke by stroke his body relaxed even more. It felt like the soft clay down by the edge of the falls and he felt his body moulding to the kneading pressure of her arms, reaching out in response to every nuance of her every touch. The passing shadow across his closed eyes alerted him to her movement as she came to kneel at his head. Gliding her oiled arms down the side of his neck, he felt them slide down either side of his spine, opening up and parting as they reached the base. He felt his buttocks tense involuntarily as her hands continued the movement over the outside of his pelvis, circled round the two mounds of taut muscle, to come together at his tail bone. This long stretch down the length of his torso meant that T'hane had to lean her full weight into the movement as she glided over his body. At the extreme of the movement her body lay out over his, her breasts and hair picking up the oil from his skin and easing the friction.

As her body moulded to his, slipping along its length and then drawing back again in strong rhythmic movements, T'hane began to lose her mind. All thoughts disappeared. She became aware only of the rhythm and the energetic connection between them as she spun his mana like silk.

Kiri allowed himself to float in the sensation. They had become as one, his body yielding to the pressure of hers, his breath and hers in unison, their minds captured together in the bliss of the sensation.

It was T'hane who returned to her senses first. Kiri probably didn't notice but her hands were not quite so sure in their touch as once again they separated to ease around his buttocks to his tail bone. This time instead of pulling them back up the spine she slid one hand a little further than the other to run down the gorge of his buttocks and around the two small mounds she found nestled in the sand like turtles eggs. Kiri felt the tingle through his body before he felt the touch of her hand. As it registered in him T'hane's hands were already on their way back up his body. Down his spine they slid again and once again paused to momentarily caress his testicles before moving on. Kiri felt his body become electric.

173

He pressed his pelvis further into the already flattened sand beneath his body as he felt himself growing. He felt his breath catch in anticipation as once again T'hane's hands snaked around his buttocks to the crease. His felt his whole body reach out in anticipation of that sweet touch but, just as she had in the water that day when she first arrived, at the last minute she swerved away, pulling her arms back up his body to his neck. He could not believe the disappointment that flooded through him. The next time her hands began the familiar path down his back he awaited again for their delicious conclusion, but once again he was disappointed. On the next stroke he had given up on her touching him there again so he was once again taken by surprise by the squeeze that she gave him before moving on.

Kiri felt his body straining to be cut loose. To be allowed to do the one, the only thing that it wanted, needed to do right now. Kiri could feel the fight inside himself. He was tired, he realised, of constantly reigning his body in. Tired of using his considerable mind power to override his desires. This time as she came around to the base of his spine, Kiri's body was alive with anticipation, yet once again she tricked him. Bringing herself up on her elbows, and with smooth rotating movements of her forearms, T'hane began working close in on either side of the spine with tiny circular motions. The weight of her body and the smallness of the contact of the elbows worked deep into the tissue and Kiri felt himself gasp, not with delight, but at the intensity of the pain. Nor did it get any lighter as she made her way up his spine to the base of his neck and it was with considerable relief that he felt her hands sweeping outwards across his shoulders to finish. Moments later he felt the sting of sharp sand in his face as T'hane rose and, as was usual after working on his body, left him stranded on the sand, bemused and deflated like a beached whale.

The effect of the last part of the massage had at least diverted his attention from his groin and left him limp and

174

useless, but just as T'hane had hoped, a small murmur of discontent was making itself heard as his body relayed the message to his mind in no uncertain terms. He wanted this woman. This was a message that was impossible to miss!

After leaving Kiri, T'hane had gone straight to the water to swim. Working on Kiri's body had been hard work. The effort of the movements added to the heat generated by the fire of desire in her abdomen, and she now burned with her own fire under the heat of the sun. The water was cool and refreshed her, but there was a part of her that this whole ocean could not quench. Turning to look at Kiri's body on the beach she saw him lazily come to his feet a little unsteadily. It had been a strong massage and his muscles felt weak like a baby. Finding his feet he looked for T'hane. His eyes found her immediately. Driven on by a surge of lust he strode toward her, as keen as she to get into the water to cool himself but, if he was honest, also driven by the need to be next to her. His body missed her touch already and was hungry for it. Lust and gluttony quickened his pace.

Warm spray rose from his feet as he entered the water. Brushing it aside, he worked his legs against its increasing resistance. Standing chest deep in the waves T'hane waited. As he came closer to her she felt compelled to move towards him. She had wanted all along that he should come to her but when it came to it and she read the intent in his eyes she wanted to meet him. Wanted it to be a decision that they both took.

The water sprayed up between them showering them in diamond shards, sending hundreds of tiny rainbows dancing around their heads. Then they were together. Their arms wrapped around each other. The embrace was so strong it took T'hane's breath for a moment. At this moment there was to be no holding back and the emotion, restrained for so long, refused to be contained any longer. It now surged forth. Both of them felt their chests would burst with the intensity of this meeting. They gulped air as if it was to be their last breath and their eyes locked in an embrace of their own.

Kiri felt the fire spring to life in his loins again and he was immediately hard against her. His hot breath warmed her cheek. Sliding his hands from her back, he brought them round to her sides and pushing up under her ribs lifted her on to him. The water aided his lift and T'hane felt herself float upward and then felt him hot inside her. It was deftly done for someone as yet unpractised she thought. Wrapping her legs around his torso she felt his pelvis move against her and her excitement build. It was an awkward position for them. Each thrust of Kiri's pelvis sent her floating upward slightly through the water and she was unable to make much movement with her own pelvis, but this wasn't just about sex. From the moment that their bodies entwined there arose in both of them an unbounded joy. It came from the tips of their toes, surged through their bodies like molten lava and, spiralling around them, lifted their spirits heavenward. It surprised and it rocked them both to their core as their souls delighted in finding one another. Suddenly out of nowhere a soft gentle rain began to fall. It was not strong enough to disturb even the surface of the water but it brought with it the gods' blessing. Separating, they made their way to the beach.

"Look," said T'hane, pointing heavenward.

A clear rainbow arch drawn across the blue sky provided yet another sign of the gods' pleasure. They felt their union blessed indeed, but not even the gods pleasure could outweigh the deep glow of contentment that Kiri felt right now. Neither one of them realised in that heady moment how much their whole being was to be forever changed by the power of Love.

They made love again as soon as they reached the beach. Falling on the soft sand, it was intense and urgent. Kiri had contained himself for so long that now he neither wanted nor indeed could hold back any longer. He had watched the islanders pleasure each other many times so the mechanics of what to do was not beyond him. Besides instinct took over where the mind failed. What he did not know, and for that matter could not have even dreamt of, was the sensation of it all. Every touch of her skin excited his body in a way that Kiri could only equate to the feeling he experienced as he built his mana. In many ways it was in fact the same. He could feel his energy grow and the release was again not dissimilar to what happened when he propelled his life force in order to crack rocks or ignite the soft green twigs with the Kahuna fire. What was so different was the fact that the whole thing happened without the concentrated use of his mind power. In fact his mind felt empty, swimming on a tide of sensation, just as it did when T'hane massaged him. Sensation after sensation flooded his body until he could sustain them no longer. He was only sorry that it was over so quickly.

That night, and indeed, every night, T'hane delighted in turning the tables on him. She became the teacher, the love Kahuna, and he the more than willing pupil. The night was her time as befits one whose 'aumakua is the owl. Easily, silently, she guided him around the secret groves of her body. She lead his hands to the soft mounds of her breasts, resting her own hands over his so that she could guide their pressure and stop their movement when she found a place especially delightful to his touch. Kiri watched her face with awe-struck curiosity and soon learnt to read its subtle messages. She taught him how to run his tongue around her nipples. Kiri was surprised to find the soft mounds becoming hard and erect to his touch. These were the things that pure voyeurism had not revealed to him. She guided his head to between her thighs to that most sacred of places. This was the most sensational discovery of all. He knew the feeling when he was inside her but the sight and the smell and the taste of her sex was a new, and yet, soon to be constant, delight to him as indeed it seemed to be for her also. Without the sight of her face to guide him, he soon learnt to gauge his efforts to her soft sighing, and to listen attentively for the catch in her breath that told him to linger in that place a little longer, but most of all he learnt to tease. In fact, he became almost as good at it as T'hane herself. His tongue even found by itself a small area at the edge of her shoulder blades that sent her into squirms of delight. He was especially pleased at this as he judged that no other had managed to find this exact place and so it was especially important to him. He may not have been her first lover but at least he had this that was unique and special to him.

T'hane also schooled him in his own pleasure. Instructing him when to delay his own release, a technique he quickly mastered; after all, he was used to containing himself. Hadn't he trained for many years in order to do just that? He never in his wildest dreams imaged that it would become so useful in circumstances such as these. By waiting, the release, when it came, was always that more intense. T'hane had a few tricks of her own that focused on his pleasure. All of the Island women had the most fluid of pelvic movements after years of performing their sacred dances. The same figure eight movements of the pelvis that she performed whilst dancing she performed on him, so that the stimulation to his penis shifted and changed, sending rivers of sensation from his groin down his legs and up into his chest. Always the tease, she would sometimes wait until his groans told her that he was near to letting go, then slide from him and leave him gasping and panting. Skipping and dancing along the waters edge she would call to her 'aumakua, giving thanks for their union and bathing in the light of the moon. On one occasion, as Kiri lifted himself on one elbow to watch her, an arc of shimmering white light formed at the edge of the beach, reaching up to the stars. Beneath it T'hane danced in the moonbow's light. She always returned to him and found him still hard and ready for her.

For awhile all thoughts of her schooling disappeared but circumstances and demands made it imperative that the lessons resume. Besides he knew that the gods had not given her to him for his own pleasure alone. There was a price for the gift he had received. The secret knowledge he had been given by Uncle could only be passed on by experience and word of mouth, and passed on it must be or it would die. A strange thing was happening however. He really began to relish the healing work that T'hane and he did together above all else. As they grew closer, his appetite for the death spells diminished. In fact, he began to experience a real resistance to their use and would pray to the 'aumakua to be released from this task. Often he would leave T'hane in her practice and go and sit on the small peninsula where he had given Uncle back to his ancestors. With the thigh bone of the old man in his lap and the dark green stone that Uncle had dropped into his hand at his death resting lightly in his palm, he ask to be released from this part of the work. His heart could no longer reconcile the delight and the pleasure of his union with another soul with the taking of life. The struggle inside him was becoming too great. Each day he would take time to sit on the lava rock and call to the ancestors.

"Oh, Mano, great hunter of the sea, just as you spared me on that day of Uncle's death, could you not also allow me the gift of sparing others? The gift of life and death we hold in our hands—can I not choose life?"

Each time the prayer went out, Kiri searched the ocean for signs of an answer. There was none. Mano, if he heard, chose to stay in the great depths. Kiri became more and more desolate. Each day of course, T'hane noticed his sadness. She saw it in the slight drop in his shoulders and the dullness in his once intense eyes. The dark dangerous aura around him was there no more, and she felt responsible. In her love and desire for this man she had robbed him of his power which was fuelled in great part by the gift of anger from the thunder god. In her he had found contentment and companionship, the like of which he never though to have. But as always the gods give and the gods take away. He was not the same man.

More and more T'hane witnessed his sadness. She too must pray to her 'aumakua for the right course of action. Her prayers of course held particular power at the time of night fall. So as the light began to fade, Kiri noticed that she would disappear into the grove of palms at the edge of the beach. There she would sit with her back against the straight trunk of a coco palm and call the owl to her. He came most nights, his bright orange eyes staring unblinking at her through the twilight. Sound came there none. As she offered her prayer for guidance to him his staring eyes gave away nothing. As she finished the prayer, on silent wings he would take to the air and in a breath he was gone. There was no answer to be had anywhere. Returning to her hut after one such fruitless excursion, T'hane threw herself on the ground in frustration. Her hand accidentally hit against something hard. Muttering a curse under her breath she reached out and picked up the object. It was the misshapen web that Kiri had given her all that time ago. In the light of recent events she had completely forgotten it and Kiri himself had not asked her about it. The twine that Kiri had used to lash the frame together had dried out and tightened and the whole structure was now rigid and hard.

"What is this thing?" she asked herself.

She turned it over in her hands looking at it first one way then another. Whichever way she looked at it, it still conveyed nothing of its possible use to her. She rolled over on to her back and held the object above her face, staring intently at its dark outline in the gloom of the hut. As she stared up at it, from the corner of her eye she glimpsed the spectacular fall of a small shower of meteors. As the stars cascaded toward the ocean she wondered at the meaning of such a display. When the gods spoke it always meant something. She turned to concentrate on the display. There were several bright glimmers of light and then the sky was still once more. T'hane loved it when the stars fell to earth. She considered it a gift from the ancient ones and a proof of their power; even though she was as yet unable to always interpret their meaning, she was always grateful nevertheless, for it meant that the gods were always near.

She returned her gaze to Kiri's web. She had been so absorbed by the light show that her arms had remained above her head holding the object whilst she watched. It took a moment to readjust her sight and accustom her eyes to the gloom in the hut once more. The web looked a little fuzzy at first and she found her gaze drawn to look through the structure rather than directly at it as she had before. Her arms were becoming tired and she lowered them slowly to regain the circulation in them. As she brought the object down before her, the background changed from that of the roof of the hut to the deep purple of the night sky just below the eaves. Between the sticks the stars twinkled. Suddenly T'hane could feel her excitement growing. She had been concentrating on the object too hard. It was not the object itself that was important, it was what it symbolized. She leapt to her feet and raced outside. Holding up the web she moved it slowly across the night sky in front of her. In a few minutes a broad smile spread across her face. The misshapen frame of sticks she realized were not as important as the shells fastened to the points where they crossed. As she looked up at one corner of the sky the shells fell exactly over the face of a group of stars. It was a map! A map of part of the night sky!

With this she surmised it would be possible to navigate across the dark waters in front of her. The gods be praised. Through the magic of the falling stars they had shown her its use at last!

More and more Kiri refused the call to perform the death spells of which he was capable. He asked the most outrageous fees for his services so that the local people were unable to comply. It was his way of getting around his increasing problem with this aspect of his work.

As the days went on and neither T'hane nor Kiri received instructions from the gods the pressure between the two of them increased. It became palpable in their every interaction. T'hane's sleep became more and more disturbed as she wrestled with her feelings of guilt. She lay down to sleep one windy night after leaving Kiri for the night. They still tended to keep to their respective huts for the majority of the night. It seemed to heighten their meeting in the mornings and besides they got more rest that way. In the distance the thunder god had awoken for the night and was murmuring his discontent. It could be a wild night she thought as she drifted fitfully in to sleep.

Suddenly there was fire everywhere. People she recognized from her village were running in every direction, bumping into each other and taking off chaotically again. Confusion and fear was palpable in the air. The palm leaf huts blazed readily, filling the air with sweet smelling, dense white smoke. Turning to her right she felt the intense heat of a blaze through the cloud of smoke and changed direction. It must have been a lightening strike. It happened occasionally. If the thunder god was especially angry he could hurl his burning spears with acute accuracy. T'hane wondered what they had done to incur his wrath. Out of the increasingly dense choking clouds of smoke, people would suddenly appear out of the night as if materialising from nowhere. If it wasn't for the screams it would have eerie indeed. T'hane realized with horror that the screaming was not that of excited villagers trying to dodge the flames and wayward sparks and shards of falling palms; in their voices she detected real terror. This was no ordinary lightening strike!

Suddenly out of the smoke a dark figure reared up towards her. She only had a moment to take in his powerful frame. What she noticed burned into her soul more intensely than the fire that she now found herself in. The man's eyes were dark and intense. His face set with a grim sneer, teeth clenched tight. Across his cheek bones and around his bottom lip and chin were dark black stains of soot rubbed into spiral designs. The tattoos gave his already frightening face an even greater impact. His eyes, opened wide with the heady mixture of fear and excitement burned into her. Around his waist was a short tapa cloth and in his right hand a large wooden club. "Warriors," she gasped. The gods were with her and the wind, suddenly changing direction, enveloped her in more smoke. She turned and ran. Although she could not see where she was running, if she kept the sound of the surf behind her she knew that she had to be heading toward the steep cliffs that enveloped the village. Her ears strained to catch the sound.

Out of the panic of fear a cool calmness suddenly descended around her as her wits returned. "Grandmother!" The old woman could not run fast to escape the marauders and T'hane guessed she would not have seen the war wakas making their way from the sea under the cover of darkness. With no shore available to pull the canoes up onto, there would not have been the warning sound of men dragging the two hulled wooden boats out of the water. They would have

183

leaped from them, weapons at the ready and attacked before anyone knew, leaving just two men with each war canoe. She could not just run and save her own skin. Stopping in her tracks she turned back towards the ocean. Again the wind had changed its mind and was now blowing the diminishing smoke out to sea. Through the grey mist that was left winding its way around the ruins of the hut and snaking up to heaven T'hane found her directions and turned towards her grandmother's hut. Her blood ran icy through her. Even at this distance she could see the still body of the old woman on the ground. Around her lay the bodies of other people that she recognized. The blood began to pound in her ears. It pounded so hard that it drowned out the screaming and the sound of the surf. All she could hear was the thump of her heart and her ragged breathing. T'hane began to run. She was sure that she was running as fast as her legs could carry her—running to be with her grandmother. The running increased the pounding in her head and her chest began to ache with the exertion.

With her heightened senses, she heard the spear before she felt it. It whistled a fine high-pitched note as it cut through the turbulent air. Many others would not have even noticed the sound, but T'hane's ears were trained to the sound of the owl on its silent night flight. She heard it's advance call, heard its deadly shriek before the kill—then her chest exploded! She felt herself propelled forward her legs still running, running, running, getting nowhere. Then she saw through a dark haze the earth rush to meet her. She didn't even feel her head hitting the ground. Around her the screaming started to fade. It sounded a long way away now. Perhaps it was over. She felt rough hands on her body. Was it her body? It didn't really feel like her body. Through her dark vision she saw an even darker face, it's eyes burning with an intensity that she had only seen once before.

"Kiri?" she said and the world went black.

The warrior stooped over her after retrieving his spear from her back. Turning her over he ran his hand down the side of her face and flicked his fingers under her chin, bringing her glazed eyes round to face him. He felt a sudden pang of remorse, not at killing her, but that he hadn't had some fun with her first. She was beautiful. A fellow warrior raced past him whooping his war cry and he stood to throw back his head and pierce the air with his victory cry. To his left the air rang with a woman's loud scream.

T'hane's scream woke Kiri. He was across the short expanse of sand and upon her before the last sound left her mouth.

"A dream, a dream," T'hane kept repeating. "By the gods, what a dream."

Kiri held her heaving body close and his strength and his warmth calmed her.

"Tell me," he said, real concern in his voice.

He knew that often the gods spoke to people in dreams. This dream concerned him greatly. He held T'hane closer to him as she told him what she had witnessed. Kiri's jaw set into a familiar pattern. T'hane was not the only one to feel fear that night.

The next day the sun burned away the residue of the night's events and Kiri continued to instruct T'hane in the ways of the Kahuna, but his mood was black. He didn't understand the dream. If the gods had spoken he didn't understand it. Was the dream a metaphor or a prophesy? Either way it wasn't good, and besides, his leg was hurting again which did nothing to enhance his already irritated mood.

For T'hane, the dream was her punishment for the guilt that she felt about Kiri. If she continued to stay and be with him, his powers might decline further, she argued to herself. The dream had pointed out to her in no uncertain terms that the gods were indeed angry with her. Here was a man whose life had been dedicated to the gods until she came along to distract him. The more she thought about it, the more obvious the dream became. Fire was the gods' punishment. She should have stayed with her grandmother. The old woman was not able to cope alone. She had as good as killed her herself. As for the warriors in the dream, well, they were nothing more than the symbols of Kiri's great temper, the legacy of the thunder god, the power of which he would surely unleash upon her if she continued to cause him distress.

A few days before the sight of the new moon T'hane came to a decision. Once taken, it tore at her insides, a monster gnawing at her vitals, yet leaving her mind numb. She had never known such pain. It was as if her heart was being ripped from her chest whilst she lived, and she felt her spirit receding as if in death. On the night of the sliver of new moon she made love with Kiri as usual, yet Kiri noticed that all the while she never took her eyes from his face. He noticed that they took in every contour, lingering most around his eyes and mouth. Once, as they gently moved against each other, she lifted one hand to run a finger over the landscape of his forehead. She traced the limits of the scar there as if seeing it were not enough, as if she had to form a tactile picture as well. As in those early days of massage on the beach, they spun their energy together, floating, sinking and swaying to its rhythm. Only one thing was missing Kiri noticed in a quite backwater of his mind. Where was the spiralling delight of the meeting of their two souls that has sealed them together that day in the water? As he drifted off toward sleep after they had rolled away from each other, he remembered her dancing in the moonbow that night and a smile spread across his face as sleep took him off. In that quiet place between wakefulness and sleep where reality merges into dream, Kiri though he heard an owl call. In the morning T'hane was gone!

T'hane had lain awake all night. Having made her decision, there would be no turning back. She had learnt so much from Kiri that would be useful to her people, but it didn't stop the pain in her stomach or ease the heavy stone in her chest where her heart once was. She had waited until a few hours before dawn before sneaking away. She could cover the ground around the beach relatively easily in the dark. She knew that she couldn't count on any help from the moon but this part off the landscape was familiar to her. By the time she reached the centre of the Island and on towards the more treacherous North shore she would have the sun to aid her. Her plan was to get as far as possible during the daylight hours of the first day, then rest for the night and be with her grandmother by the fading light of the next day.

At the onset of her journey she made good time as she progressed deeper into the grove of trees that backed the beach. Out of the noises of the night she heard the lone cry of an owl and felt comforted by the eerie sound. It was good to know that her 'aumakua was with her. Moving easily, her mind numbed to all thought that might distract her from her chosen mission, she peered ahead intently to make out the pathways between the trees. The bird came out of nowhere making her cry out in surprise. Swooping in low from her left, she felt the tip of its wing brush the top of her head. Banking steeply, the owl alighted on the ground in front of her, it's staring eyes looking straight at her. She had never seen the bird behave in this way before. Normally the 'aumakua of the air only touched the ground briefly to latch on to their tiny prey. When resting they preferred the advantage of a high perch where their great saucer eyes could look for slight movements below that would alert them to food. More importantly, they needed a clear open advantage point with which to pick up the most minute of sounds enabling them to locate their prey where even their sharp eyes could not see. The bird sat motionless. T'hane bowed her head.

"Thank you, Kūkauakahi, for accompanying me," she said. "I am honoured by your presence on my journey."

The owl remained still. T'hane was unsure as to how to proceed, but proceed she must if she was to keep to her self-allotted schedule. She took the owl's presence in front of her as an indication that she should change direction and find another path. Maybe the path ahead had been washed away in the evening storms, she thought. It did happen, and she did not want to find herself having to come back on her self to find a clearer route through. So with that in mind, and asking the gods' forgiveness, she started to walk off to her left. The owl rose from the ground. The initial sound of his takeoff was immediately followed by silence as he soared up into the trees. Again T'hane was surprised by his diving flight, this time just in front of her face. On this occasion he did not come to rest on the ground but banked away out of sight.

"Strange," T'hane muttered to herself.

Above her she heard his plaintive cry and then, a few seconds after, an answering call behind her. Back and forth the call went. T'hane wondered what had disturbed them so, but she quickened her pace as she noticed that the trees ahead were becoming clearer in the first light of the new day. Coming out onto clear ground she stopped for a moment to draw breath. Out of the trees and soaring high into the sky above her she saw the two birds. They circled one another for a while then raced at each other. Locked together, claw on claw, they spiralled around each other, descending all the time toward the earth. As they reached a few feet above T'hane's upturned face one bird broke away to fly across her from the left hand side. As it come closer, T'hane noticed its orange eyes locked on to her. The body of the owl was making tiny adjustments to its flight path, its body seeming to rotate around the disc of its stationary, immobile head. He was in attack mode.

At that moment T'hane realised that she was the bird's target. She saw his claws swing forward, stretched out in front of him ready to lock on, his eyes never leaving hers. Instinct made her duck, but even so she felt his talons dig into the top of her head, and she winced at the tug on her hair as the bird climbed skyward again, his claws sliding through her sleek locks. Hardly recovering from this attack she saw, out the corner of her eye, the second bird already swooping in on her. She raised her arms to protect her head and face. The bird's claws drew blood.

T'hane was now distraught. Never had she been attacked in this manner. The owl was her 'aumakua, her protector; and now here were two of them diving at her and even attacking her. This was an obvious omen but one that she felt she had little time to consider. Was she to return to the beach, back to Kiri, back to her guilt? Perhaps she was not to return to her village. She would certainly have a lot of explaining to do to grandmother, and then there would be the shame of not finishing her training. After all, she was not yet initiated as a true keeper of the secrets. She felt trapped, unable to return, yet unsure as to how to proceed.

"I have no choice," she whispered as much to the owls as to herself. "I have to go to my village. There is nowhere else for me to go." A sudden great wave of sadness enveloped her.

When Kiri awoke and could not find T'hane, he was not at first unduly concerned, but he did become more and anxious as the morning wore on. He knew there were many places she could be. He knew that collecting herbs was one of her favourite pastimes. There were some herbs that she said were more potent picked by the light of the moon or when the early morning dew was still upon the leaves. His best idea was that she was content somewhere collecting her fresh supplies and would be home soon. She had been different last night as they had lain together: sad, he thought, and pensive. He had been unable to read her mind effectively, but he guessed it had something to do with his moods of late. Why, when he counted himself so fortunate, he still allowed these dark thoughts to perturb him he didn't know.

As the sun rose farther in the sky so did his concern. He tried to tune his mind into hers. What he received disturbed him. He could sense anxiety, but no real thoughts formed in his mind. Her mind was a blank to him.

She was blocking him. He decided to visit the sharks. Maybe they would have some advice for him at this time. Making his way to the familiar spot on the peninsula he sat down quietly at the water's edge and closed his eyes. As he quieted his thoughts all was still for a while. He focused on drawing the fresh sea breeze into his lungs, allowing it to refresh and revive him. The sun, not yet at its full force, warmed his face and eased the tension from his forehead and neck. He was aware of the dull ache in his leg but it was like an old friend now, always around, yet not intruding to the point of distraction. The sound of the ocean spoke to him and trance-like he rose from his position and decided he needed to swim—needed to immerse himself in the element of his ancestors—to allow the waters to support and nourish him. The warm ocean welcomed him and wrapped itself around him. He rolled over on his back and allowed the water to hold him in its rocking embrace. Floating relaxed, he let the tension ease out of his muscles as the ocean coaxed him to let go. It would be so easy, he thought, just to let go of it all, just to give in. The pull of the ancestors was strong!

A stray strip of weed slid over his abdomen as he lay cushioned in the ocean's embrace and his body at once remembered that first day in the water with T'hane. A small point of longing emerged in his chest. Behind his closed eyes he could see her bright face framed with Hau flowers. Suddenly her face disappeared and in its place came the sight of fire. T'hane's dream!

Of course, he thought. It is so obvious, she has returned home. The dream warned of something befalling her grandmother; it is only right that she would heed this omen and return to the old woman.

His mind relaxed a little as he made this connection, but down in the pit of his stomach a small, icy-cold worm was squirming around his insides, and he felt his abdomen tense involuntarily. He decided that he, too, would go to T'hane's village. If the old woman was ill or some disaster had befallen the village then he could be of help. Besides he missed T'hane so much.

Deciding not to set out in the high part of the sun's path across the top of the sky, he spent the rest of the morning collecting a few herbs and ti leaves that would come in useful. As he was leaving, he felt compelled to also pick up the thigh bone of Uncle and the small green stone that he had given him at his death. For good measure he also placed his new conch shell into the tapa bag which he slung over his shoulder.

You never know, he thought.

T'hane had made good time to the village and did indeed arrive well before nightfall of the second day after she had set out from Kiri's home. Grandmother had been delighted and yet surprised to meet with her grand daughter. The old woman had given her a hearty welcome, setting some of the day's catch of fish in ti leaves and burying them in the hot embers of the day's fire. While they waited for the fish to cook, T'hane told her grandmother something of her new life. Without giving anything away she told how she could now take away pain and heal broken bones in the time it took to light a fire. She told of the experiences with the thought forms that could possess people, draining their life force and causing a slow and often painful death. Her grandmother had seen these things in her long life, but of course she did not know to take them away and had sat for long hours with hapless souls watching their slow demise. They laughed together as T'hane told some, but not all, of Kiri and her sexual exploits. She lingered over the areas where she could show grandmother that her expert tuition had been put to good use and was much appreciated. The old woman threw back her head and roared with laughter and delight at T'hane's stories. The fish was overcooked before they took it from its charred wrapping and ate it steaming hot with their fingers. Time had slipped by without them even noticing.

As the darkness enveloped the village the two women bade each other goodnight. Grandmother took T'hane's face in her hands and pressed her forehead to hers, their noses lightly touching. She knew that T'hane had not told all of the story but she would get more, no doubt, tomorrow.

Before she herself lay down for the night, she took her small pouch of stones and laid it on the ground before her. In a low deep voice she began to call her 'aumakua. Almost immediately a large owl came out of the dusk and alighted on her hut. Manu took the stones from the pouch and cupped them in her hands. Blowing on them with her breath, she shook them for several moments. Holding them to her chest she then threw them to the ground in front of her. Running her

192

hands over the arrangement of stones she began to read their message. The picture emerging through her fingers caused them to shake. As she received more of the message contained within them the blood began to sink from her face and the cold grip of fear took its hold. Manu felt Kūkauakahi reach out to her and her soul respond. She knew, but could not understand, that death was at her shoulder and the call of her ancestors rang loud in her ears!

Kiri made his way purposefully through the trees. He knew he had several hours of daylight left and wanted to cover as much ground as possible before the night made travel impossible. His leg was catching every so often as he made his way over the uneven ground. Several times he stopped to rub it vigorously which seemed to help for a while. Then the ache was back again. It seemed to be growing sharper for no obvious reason. Kiri remembered that the old wound troubled him most at times when it was imperative for him to be alert. It was a sort of warning call from the gods. He felt uneasy and lengthened his stride.

That night he decided to light a fire. It wasn't cold but he wanted its company as the night, with just it's sliver of moon, was inky black. He was pleasantly tired after his walk and was looking forward to sleep. He stretched out with his back against a large sloping rock. It was still warm from the day's heat and gave his back enough support to ensure at least a few hours sleep. As he settled himself, glancing briefly at the last embers of his fire, his nostrils picked up a scent. A scent was too strong a word, in fact, for what Kiri's trained nose was registering. Far off in the distance, so that Kiri only caught whiffs of it, he could smell rain. This in itself was not unusual. Rain came to the Island most nights. But this rain had a different quality to it. It was more robust, more pungent, and when Kiri tuned into the skin on the back of his arms he could feel them beginning to stand alert to the shift in the pressure of the atmosphere. Storm, he thought to himself. I hope it doesn't break before I get to the village in the morning.

The morning came, as it usually did, with a broad sunny smile and Kiri set off again as soon as he could see the face of the sun over the horizon. The heat would not pick up for several hours and his body felt good. The warm stone had ensured that his muscles had stayed relaxed, the rain had not materialised and he had slept well. The journey on proceeded without incidence, yet Kiri was aware of a slight freshening in the air, and his nostrils tingled as they tried to detect the change in the weather. When he was close to the North Shore he scanned the horizon for storm clouds. The sky was clear. Just before the descent to the village there was a dry cave that Kiri knew. He had already decided to spend the night there before attempting the steep climb down to T'hane's grandmother's home at daybreak. The cave was not big. It would hold maybe ten men with ease. At its mouth Kiri could stand easily but it sloped dramatically back from the rock face so that the only way to reach the interior was on hands and knees. After eating a supper of fruit he crawled into the cave. There was no need for a fire tonight, and the soft sand beneath him would provide a comfortable enough place to sleep. He thought briefly that he heard the murmur of the thunder god, but if he did it was a long way off and Kiri decided not to pay it too much attention. After all he was a common enough visitor in these parts.

It was impossible to tell at what time Kiri was awakened. The cave seemed to be even darker than the night itself. Tucked deep inside as he was, the outside was shut off from him. All sounds of the night were deadened by the solid walls. It was Kiri's nose that woke him. This time it was not the smell of a distant storm that wafted across his face but the sweet, musty smell of smoke.

Strange, his mind mused, still lazy with sleep, the village

194

fires should be dampened down now for the night. Once his brain had been sufficiently roused by the smoke he was immediately alerted to the unmistakable sound of screaming. Scrambling to the mouth of the cave, kicking sand over himself in his haste so that he had to shake himself on reaching the open, he stood very still and listened. Now very distinctly, carried through the still night air, came the clouds of smoke and the frightening wail of women and the angry shouts of men. Kiri felt a surge of red hot anger fill his body and explode in his head. He had to get down to the village, down to T'hane, and the dark was not going to stop him. Taking the bone of Uncle from the bag which he then slung across his back, he waved the bone in front of him as he made his way to the edge of the cliff. Moving like a blind man he was able to proceed at some pace, stopping only when the bone made contact with something so that he had to feel his way around the obstacle before proceeding. Things became a lot more hazardous once he began the descent. Often his feet would go from beneath him and he would flail about until his hand could grasp a low bush strong enough to halt his descent and allow him to catch his breath. Sometimes the bush would prove too weak and it would come away in his hand, sending showers of earth and small stones over him. His back, too, was assaulted by jutting rocks buried none too deeply in the earth. But the pain meant nothing. Pain he could deal with. What he found more difficult to deal with was the thought of what might be happening below him. That the cries and shouts he had heard were made by warriors, he had no doubt. The purpose of their attack was more of a mystery, although often these men had no more reason to mount a raid on a village other than to prove their loyalty and their bravery to their chief.

"Their bravery!" he spat out with a mouthful of dirt. "Is it brave to attack such a small community under cover of night for no real purpose?"

It seemed an eternity before Kiri reached the edge of the slope on the outskirts of the village. The sky was just beginning to lighten and the horizon was shot through with dark purple and blood-red streaks. Kiri paused to calm his breathing. Staring at the sky he saw the omen clearly. The sky was bleeding and, away to his right, an immense dark black bruise of cloud was forming as he watched. He could still hear the shouts but the screaming was no more and the thick smoke was thinning. Half running, half crouching, he made his way to where he could get a clearer view of the village and the open sea. What he saw took his legs from under him and he sank to his knees in the earth. There was not a soul standing as his eyes took in the view in front of him. Men lay with their fishing spears in their hand, their only weapons. Their heads were smashed like coconuts, the already ochre earth stained deeper red with their blood. Many of the women's bodies lay to the edges of the compound with the children where they had been slain as they tried to escape. There had been no chance of survival for any of them. The attack had been swift and deadly. Slowly forcing his body to respond, Kiri lifted his eyes to the sea. There he saw three large war waka, sails hoisted to take advantage of the stiffening offshore breeze. The fire inside him turned ice cold. Kiri fought with every fibre of his body to control the rage in the pit of his stomach.

Getting to his feet he began to walk through the bodies strewn on the ground. His mind raced. There was nothing to say that T'hane was here, he told himself. He had only guessed that she had made her way to her grandmothers, perhaps he was wrong.

"Oh, by the gods, let me be wrong," he said aloud.

His head was swimming, drowning in a mixture of rage and fear. The stench of blood and burned flesh assailed his nostrils and his eyes were glazed with tears from the stinging smoke.

196

He knew before he reached her that it was her. She was lying apart from the others, more towards the edge of the camp where the other women had fallen, but instead of facing away from the carnage as they were caught in flight for their lives, she was lying flat on her back, her face to the morning sun as if catching its first light before waking. Kiri had seen her lie this way so many times. This time, however, he knew that she would not roll to her side and give her beaming smile to him as she heard him make his way to her to welcome both her and the new day. His legs did not want to carry him. They became stiff and unwilling. His mind screamed silently and his breath refused to leave his lungs, so devastated was he by what he saw. Again his mind fought to reassure. He could see no wound—perhaps she lived. Perhaps she was just stunned and at any moment would move and the nightmare would be over.

As he stumbled towards where she lay he could feel all hope receding. Kneeling beside her, he reached out a cautious hand to touch her face. There was no response. Overwhelmed he reached toward her and lifted her body to his in an embrace. The sticky, blood soaked earth clung to her back and he almost recoiled in horror before his mind reminded him that this was T'hane. Her lifeless body felt alien to him. The spark that flowed so readily between them was no longer there; there was no response to his touch. Her spirit had gone. Only the serene beauty of her face remained. Kiri began to cry quietly. At first the tears fell silently down his cheeks and into her hair; then as he could hold them in no longer, great sobs escaped him as he gently rocked her like a child. At that moment his heart broke. He felt it snap in his chest; felt the numbness replace it as the grief swept over him fighting like a caged animal desperate to be free. It rose from his bowels and seized him by the throat, choking him and leaving him fighting for breath, struggling with the fierce constriction in his throat. Holding her close to him, he felt her breasts pressed against his chest, her abdomen resting lightly on his as it had done so many times before. With slow deliberation he stroked his hand through her hair. Through his crazed grief, the Kahuna in him divined her burst heart where the spear had spent its force. Yet it was no more broken than his.

Then his mind divined something else, a small barely perceptible pin point of mana. Puzzled, he relaxed his hold and let T'hane's body fall away from him. Staring in disbelief, he placed his hand on her abdomen. The grief held in the tortuous lock in his throat would be contained no longer. With mind numbing realization, he registered the last ebb of mana from the tiny soul in the body of his love and his heart broke all over again. The wail that finally escaped him carried like a siren on the wind. Bouncing off the walls of the steep slopes, it reverberated back to him so that the land itself shared in his anguish. Grabbing her to him again he continued to wail until his throat was hoarse and he had only the energy to sob dry heaving breaths that left his chest raw inside with the wound of his love.

For an eternity he held her. He could not let her go, could not be parted from her—could not bear to allow himself to feel the loneliness again. Looking down into her face he said quietly.

"T'hane, my love. All the secrets of my art I shared with you and yet the most important secret I held back. I am so sorry. I never told you how much I love you, little one."

He was suddenly reminded of the times that he had spoken harshly to her and the times when he withheld his praise for her labours at the learning of the chants or her initiative at working with the sick. Suddenly, as if his body said that it could purge itself no more, he felt a quiet peace descend upon him. Gently laying T'hane's body back on the earth he got to his feet. He felt shaky but clearer.

"T'hane," he said out loud over her. "Know that I love you more than life, and that somehow I will find a way of letting you know. Somehow you must know what you mean to me. By all the gods I shall find a way. I will love you forever. This I promise."

Pulling himself away from her, he headed in the direction of Manu's hut or at least the area where her hut should have been. The old woman was lying in the scorched remains, her legs badly burned by the fallen roof. In death her hand was clenched around the tiny skull at her throat. She had been praying to her ancestors at the last. Turning away from her, Kiri's toe caught something hard half buried in the sand. Cursing under his breath he looked down to see the conch shell that he had given to Manu when he had come to her that day to ask that T'hane might accompany him back to his home to be his apprentice. He stooped to pick it up. He felt the slight tingle in his hands. It still retained his mana. Brushing the sand from it he laid it carefully to one side and then returned to T'hane. Lifting her, he carried her across to where Manu lay and placed her along side her Grandmother. Then taking a little of the 'awa that he always carried in his bag he offered it to the gods and then began to chant. His voice was shaking and he was struggling to remember the words that would summon the ancestors and aid the journey of their two souls to the 'aumakua. As the chant proceeded, he felt his energy return, and soon the words came out loud and strong and the power filled him.

When he was finished he sat in silence before the two women. He had done what was necessary. He could do no more for them other to arrange for men to come and to bury them, and all the others, in the manner of their tribe. This he would do. But there was something else that he had to do first. Picking up the shell, Kiri turned and began to make his way back up the deep slopes to the top of the cliffs where he could get the best view of the disappearing waka.

Strong will and determination carried him to the top of the cliff speedily. Shielding his eyes from the glare of the sun, he found the three dark specks on the water. The strengthening breeze had taken them far out to sea. This was not going to be easy.

Kiri dropped on one knee and took the shell from his bag. Pressing his lips to it he drew in a deep breath through his nose and blew through the small hole specially bored at one end. A deep rich call came from the shell. It was picked up by the wind and carried out to sea. Two more times he let the shell alert the attention of the gods. Then breathing deeply to increase his mana, Kiri began to call on the ancestors. First he called to his own 'aumakua, the shark, and then the 'aumakua of T'hane and Manu, the owl. He asked for their help, asked for their power in the deed he had to perform. Then once again putting the shell to his lips he let the call travel out across the sea again. Taking Uncle's thigh bone he began to strike the earth. For the deed he had in mind he would need the power of as many of the gods as he could muster to his cause. Finally, he began to concentrate his mana in his head, more specifically in the front of his head. With all his concentration he focused every bit of power available to him at this point until the dark mark of the thunder god on his forehead began to pulse violently. Of all the gods it was this one that Kiri needed most, for the deed he was about to perform was dark indeed.

Suddenly he felt the air grow thick around him and a pressure began to build up at his back. He locked his feet to the earth to brace himself against its push. Then whilst he fought to contain it, he felt the presence move into him from behind. He felt his body swell as the power filled him. He seemed to be growing—getting taller and wider by the moment. A dark cloud or energy enveloped him and settled finally around his head. The rage in his abdomen was so intense he felt he would burst. The thunder god had answered the call and was with him. In confirmation, off in the distance, a loud rumble filled the air.

Kiri realized that the first thing he had to do was change the wind. The strong offshore breeze was keeping the storm far out on the horizon and that was the last place he wanted it. With the power of the thunder god in him, he focused his mind, and under his breath began to talk with the wind. If the wind was listening, there was no sign of it understanding. Kiri was still aware of it blowing out to sea. He had spoken with the wind on many occasions in the past. They had had many playful conversations and it had been cooperative many times in helping the fishing boats put out to sea and in bringing them safely home again. Only this time it was no fishing trip that Kiri wanted to influence and he had no intention of the inhabitants of these particular boats coming home safely! Maybe the wind would not help in this instance, Kiri thought. He dismissed the thought immediately. He would not be deterred from his task. Turning his focus to the gathering dark clouds at the horizon, he appealed to the thunder god again. Again the god responded. After all, Kiri was his chosen one. When asked for help the gods had to respond, and Kiri was counting on this fact. As Kiri continued to will the wind to change and the storm to come closer he suddenly felt the wind falter. At first it hesitated, swirling around him in confusion. It seemed unsure, halting even. The intensity died down and the air stilled. Out on the ocean the waka sails began to flap uncontrollably as the wind died. The crew worked to bring the sails in as they were becalmed.

Out on the horizon the thunder god matched Kiri's rage. As Kiri watched the black clouds began to move slowly closer toward him. He could feel the touch of a small breeze on his face and then the increase pressure as the wind began to blow against him. Like an angry army the clouds rode in on the wind. As they advanced Kiri could see lightening illuminating the inside of the clouds so that they momentarily glowed grey

201

and pink before the sky turned electric blue as the lightening bolt let loose to dive in to the waters. The thunder god roared his approval at every strike. Soon the clouds began to join forces until the whole face of heaven was wearing the angry countenance of the thunder god. Then there came the rain. Kiri saw it drop from the clouds in sheets until the cloud itself looked as if it dipped into the ocean, drawing up more water to replenish itself in a continuous, inexhaustible cycle.

Kiri was one with the power. The god was in him and around him. He felt his force and he was exalted. With every lightening strike he rejoiced, shouting encouragement into the wind until the words came back to sting in his face. At that moment he was a god and the elements were at his command. Out on the ocean, death came quickly to the warriors. The waters opened up for them and the sharks completed Kiri's revenge.

It was done! He who had begged the gods to let him choose life had chosen death. In sorrow he realised those two giants would always be a part of him. Thus it was with all men.

The strain of exacting not only the death spell, but controlling the power of the 'aumakua and the natural elements, took it's toll, and Kiri saw the world swirling before his eyes as his legs finally gave way and he sank to the ground unconscious. For a while everything was black as he hovered somewhere in the void between life and death. It was with regret that he found himself stirring and once again becoming aware of the horror of the previous night. The stone in his heart had been joined by another in the pit of his stomach. Without warning he was violently sick. The meagre contents of his last meal of fruit meant that there was not much to bring up, but nevertheless he continued to retch, bringing up thick green bile, that burned his throat and nose. It was as if his body was trying to rid itself of all the hate and disgust held deep inside him. He continued to retch kneeling on all fours like a dog until his diaphragm ached with the effort and his sterile efforts brought forth no more. He was weak. He had to rest and then find help to administer to the dead. Like an animal he made his way to the dry cave again, and wrapping his body in a tight ball, hugged his legs to his chest as he lay on his side in the sand. Rocking gently he fell asleep.

It was a troubled sleep. Vivid pictures kept springing to the front of his mind causing him to toss and turn and cry out.

T'hane's face.

Her blood on his hands.

Strange dark faces, twisted in agony.

Manu's hand clasped around the tiny skull.

Fire.

T'hane's face.

The gaping jaws of a shark.

Lightening.

T'hane's face and the sound of his name on her lips.

He woke with a start, his breath coming in short pants. He sat up and rested his head against the wall of the cave. It was cool. Suddenly the horror of the attack paled as the realization of what he had done dawned on him. All the while that he and T'hane had been together, he had taken a vow not to work the death spell. The love that flowed between them poured into the work that they did with the sick. There was no place for vengeance. He had refused others when they had come to him to ask him to exact revenge on their behalf and yet he had felt nothing as he took his revenge for T'hane's death. What was more, he had enlisted the help of the 'aumakua in his task. He had failed. Failed T'hane, failed the ancestors and more than that failed himself. He did not deserve to live. Throwing back his head he called out to the gods to take him and waited for what he hoped would be their swift reply.

But the gods did not take him. The weeks after T'hane's death passed painfully slowly for Kiri. He went about his daily tasks in a daze. Nothing he did had meaning for him. His faith was gone, turned to cold anger at the gods for allowing T'hane to be taken from him. The gods had brought them together and then taken her from him. It felt like a cruel joke. It was not the act of a loving akua and he wanted nothing more to do with them.

After T'hane's death, he had pulled down the hut that he had made for her. He could not bear the thought of waking each morning to look across at it and not see her body stretching out to greet the day in that slow languid way that he found so enticing. Every part of the hut he had burned. Standing, watching the smoke rise into the air, his nostrils reminded him of the carnage at T'hane's village. He never returned to that place after he and the others had buried the dead in the manner of their tribe. He knew, of course, where her bones lay. He had no desire to return to them when time had stripped them bare and to bring them back to his home as was the custom in several places on the Island. He knew that to the other islanders her spirit resided in her skeleton. He had no doubt that if she had had surviving family they would have taken her bones to revere, lavishing love and attention on them to please her departed spirit. Kiri had no need or desire for such things. T'hane's spirit lived on deep inside him. It was a part of his being. Not a day went by when she wasn't in his head. His loins still ached for her touch, and his mind saw her in every shadow. As he fell asleep each night, the cry of the owl bid him goodnight. He took to waiting for it, drawing comfort from the sad note in its voice.

"Good night," he would whisper. "Sleep well, little one."

Often as not the nightly rain would then begin to fall and his mind would relax.

The story of the decimation of the people on the North Shore and Kiri's revenge on the marauding warriors spread around his community. He could not imagine that anyone had witnessed the event and he himself had spoken to no one. Yet they knew. He could sense them talking about him in hushed whispers, and he knew that the story fed their fear of him even more. They avoided him, and his loneliness became more and more painful because of it.

Sometimes he sought solace in the arms of Pele, journeying in his mind to where the fire goddess poured her fiery liquid into the ocean. With his inner eye he would look down through the clear waters at the river of red as it bubbled and burst its way through the black stone. The water boiling and steaming in turmoil matched his own agitation. The earth, it seemed, was bleeding; but in that very act Kiri knew it was creating new life to the land.

More and more, however, he took time out, usually towards the end of the day after the last meal, to go and sit on the peninsula. It was here by his ancestors that he felt most at peace. Time rolled on unceasingly like the ocean.

Over time, the pain of loss did not abate. Kiri became resigned to the fact that his life went on. The gods were not ready to receive him and so he must continue. As he sat one early morning with the ancestors at the edge of the peninsula, watching the fins cutting through the water in lazy circles, an insight became apparent to him and a solemn vow was taking place inside him. With increased clarity he realized that the techniques for mana building and the projection of energy he was so skilled in, in order to affect the death spell, could be changed, just subtly, to heal instead of kill. It was so obvious to him that he chastised himself for not realising it sooner. Just like the powerful herbs that grew on the Island, which T'hane would gather to make into potions for healing, differing quantities could heal or harm or even bring death. So it was not such a giant leap of imagination to recognize that his energy techniques could do likewise. Could not the spear be used to catch fish to feed the hungry as well as to kill one's enemies. The spear was but the instrument, the mind and the consciousness of the thrower was what determined the outcome.

He also realised that he had to move. He no longer wished to stay in the place that held so many painful memories for him. Sometimes the grief would overwhelm him, paralysing him for days at a time. At these times his whole body was racked with pain. It ached for T'hane's touch with a passion and an intensity that set every fibre of his being on fire. It grabbed at his breath and squeezed his heart within a inch of his very life. He wasn't sure that he could carry on. During these times he turned to the 'awa for help. Lying on the warm sand, he would keep drinking until the numbness in his mouth and throat percolated through his entire body and eventually reached his mind.

He decided that he would move to the North Shore, not to the site of T'hane's village, but somewhere along that stretch of coastline. He liked the rugged intensity of it and it somehow suited his mood more than the calm of his beach. The decision to move gave him renewed energy. He would find a new place.

He took very little with him, the bone of Uncle, of course, and the green rock that he had given him, the conch shell and his kukui nut lei. He hesitated long and hard over the small wooden bowl that T'hane had ground her herbs in. In the end he took it. Some nights he would fall asleep with it pressed to his cheek. If he imagined really hard he could feel her cheek in the warm smoothness of the wood and the faint lingering sense of her mana.

Once he was settled in his new hut, nestled against the top of the high finger cliffs of the North shore, he set to work perfecting the techniques necessary for instantaneous healing and for cleansing the bones of old patterns of energy that could cause disease. Most of all, he perfected the ways for healing the poor souls of his fellow people, who, like him, had lost faith and been cut off from the love and support of the 'aumakua and were crying out for help to re-establish that vital connection. This aspect of the work that he had created brought him a special pleasure, for it seemed to him an act of restitution for the devastation that he had reeked on that fateful day all those months ago, and for turning his back on the gods. Angry as he was with them, he realized that he could no more live without their love than without the air in his lungs. The work was the only joy in his life and for a while he was able to push his great loneliness aside although he could never rid himself of it completely.

He didn't know how long it was after T'hane's death that he received the insight to take another apprentice. The work he had developed along with the other skills passed to him from Uncle had, of course, to be passed on. This, he concluded, was the reason the gods had not listened to his pleas to be taken from this life after T'hane's death. The skills he had had to be taught through example, just as he had learned all those years ago. This time, though, the death spell would be missing from his teaching. He would continue to teach the art of depossession, as there seemed to be such a call for it amongst the islanders, for whilst he had turned his back on such arts there were many Kahuna 'anā'anā who had not. With mixed feelings he put it out to the gods that he was ready for a new pupil and awaited their reply. It was slow in coming, but one evening as the sun completed his journey for the day and prepared to slip into the waters to travel to the far side of the earth to be born again the next day, a stranger appeared on the cliff path. Kiri watched as the figure made its way toward him where he sat in front of his hut. He knew before any word was spoken; before any contact was made, that this would be his new pupil, and once again he found himself cursing the gods for their choice.

"Not a woman!" he cursed.

She was fortunately unlike T'hane in almost every way. Smaller in stature and older, Kiri noticed that she too had a small dark mark of the thunder god upon her neck. She had spirit, this he knew, for these days no one sought him out unless they were truly desperate. She came with a request, innocuous at first, for a love spell. As he spoke with the woman however it became obvious that the purpose of such a spell was not to procure the love of another for herself, but to slip it to a man that she felt had mistreated her so that he fell in love with the woman of his brother. In this way she wished to create havoc for the man and have him cast out from his own family. It was a small act of revenge in comparison to Kiri's, but revenge never the less. He talked her out of the love spell and, in return for her long walk to find him, promised to teach her a little magic of her own. He could tell by the look in her eyes that she was hooked. He also knew that it wasn't going to be easy.

Even before they began to work together in earnest her temper would flare and, often as not, he would be the recipient of it. She was stubborn and reactive. She lacked the sense of fun that he had so enjoyed about T'hane. But she was also determined and a hard worker and after a while Kiri decided that she was after all a worthy pupil.

The teaching kept him occupied, and it was good to have the companionship of another human in his life again. It was not enough to stop the pain of his grief from rearing up, however, and as time progressed he grew more and more weary of spirit. The nightly greeting of the pueo was a constant reminder of T'hane. In fact, since this new woman had begun her apprenticeship, it seemed the owl's cry had become more and more insistent. He still missed her so much.

Despite her constant arguments, his pupil was progressing well, and he knew that the time of her 'ailolo ceremony was approaching. He remembered back to his own initiation and felt the warm flood of emotion in his chest as he remembered Uncle. He was pleased to have been able to pass his skills on to this woman. It meant that the secrets of his trade would continue on, probably through women, he mused. After all it was women who seemed to possess a natural aptitude for healing. It was they who were in touch with the seed power of creation and sensitive to the many moods of the moon and the ocean. Besides, his current apprentice had exhibited a powerful antagonism towards the men she had contact with, him included! He felt sure that she would pass the knowledge on to another female.

The day of the 'ailolo approached and as Kiri sat by the ocean watching the waters turn from blue to black in the fading light, a great tiredness came over him. It reached deep inside him and touched his very bones. No, it touched his very spirit. He had fulfilled his obligation to pass on his knowledge only to one who would also guard the secrets of the craft until she herself found one worthy to pass them on to. His work was done, and he realized that he had no desire to continue in life. Why, indeed, should he continue to live when T'hane was gone, and when he had taken the lives of so many others in revenge. His task was complete, his obligation honoured, his restitution fulfilled. He felt suddenly old. Out of nowhere great tears welled from his eyes and rolled down his face. He tasted their ocean saltiness on his lips. He wanted to go home.

No self-respecting Kahuna would put his pupil to the task of the 'ailolo ceremony until they were ready and their success assured. There was always a slight edge of doubt however. The ceremony was in the hands of the gods. The final decision to accept a Kahuna was always with them. In this case, as was Kiri's hope, his pupil was accepted. Of course, after the initiation there was the feast. The pig, having been offered to the gods for the ceremony, was then to be devoured. Kiri ate well. He like the feeling of fullness and weight in his belly. So often he felt empty inside by contrast and not with the lack of food. The pig tasted sweet and the hot fat ran down his arms and chin as he tore the flesh from the bone and stuffed it into his mouth. He had made fresh 'awa for the ceremony and, as none could be left over, for it had been consecrated to the ancestors, he had finished what was left in the gourd. He could feel its affects taking over his senses. When he could eat no more, he decided to make his way to ocean. He felt a little unsteady on his feet as he made his way across the cliff top and began the descent. There was a warm breeze blowing in off the ocean, and he let it caress his cheeks which felt sticky and tight from the pig fat. Low on the horizon a giant moon was floating. Kiri let his gaze fall on its face. The moon weaved her magic and he became mesmerised by her beauty. Out of the corner of his eye he could see the figure of a woman swirling and dancing in the moonlight, and softly in his ear the sound of her prayer for thanks to her 'aumakua wove around his brain. From the spot on the beach where she danced, a fine shimmer of white light arched up into the night sky, reaching back to its mother, the moon. Forcing his gaze away from the moon's face, Kiri turned his face toward the figure. The moonbow still glowed with its ghostly light, but there was no other soul there.

His stone heart lurched in his chest.

"T'hane!" he shouted as if she had just danced out of sight. He desperately wanted her to return. Oh, how desperately he wanted her to return.

His heart weighing heavier than ever in his chest, he eventually reached the water's edge. The soft swell of the ocean made his head swim. He was having difficulty focusing his eyes. As had happened often before, sometimes in that half world between waking and sleeping, a procession of images floated before him.

The dark face of an unknown woman, close to his.

Uncle writhing in the frenzy of the death spell.

A child being born.

T'hane's face.

Rock cracking and opening up in front of him.

Storm clouds and lightening.

Sharks' fins cutting the water.

Manu's head thrown back in laughter.

Her lifeless body in the embers of the fire.

War canoes in a boiling sea.

The wide staring eyes of the owl.

This last image stayed with him, two orange moons mesmerizing him. As he stared into the orbs he heard the bird's cry behind him as he did every night.

He wanted to be in the water. His mind told him that he needed to wash the pig fat from his body, but his spirit wanted to be cradled in the ocean's calm embrace. He wanted, as he had so many times before, to just let go and let the ocean take care of him. Let it wash over him, soothing his pain and lifting the hurt from his body. He slipped into the dark waters. His skin sighed at its warm silkiness. His mind was still woozy from the 'awa, and his body, which had felt full and heavy on land now felt more comfortable. He turned on his back and floated, absorbed in the motion of the waves.

He didn't know how long he stayed like that, eyes half closed, lazily watching the moon break free from the bonds of the earth and float higher and higher into the sky. He suddenly wanted to swim. He wanted to work his body. Swivelling onto his front he started to swim out with easy, strong strokes. It felt good. He was always at home in the water and he enjoyed the way his body cut through the surface with practiced ease. On and on he swam his body growing in strength with each stroke through the water. On and on he went, far out from the shelter of the land. Out to where he could feel the ocean's pull on him—feel it's deep undercurrents.

Suddenly, the black silhouette of a fin joined him. It paced him as he moved through the water. Then the one dark fin became two, and then three, and four, and then five. They swam in formation, two on either side of him and one riding the waves in front of him.

Kiri was aware of the current produced by its powerful body rippling back to him over the pull of the ocean beneath him. As he continued to swim, his mind began to join with the 'aumakua at his left side. Even in the dark he noticed the white mark just behind its head. His consciousness changing, he thought that he began to feel the way the water split around the shark's head, to flow as two spiralling currents around its sleek body. He was suddenly acutely aware of the sides of his body becoming sensitive to the slight currents and vibrations of the other sharks as they powered through the water beside him. His mouth moved in a wide grin. His legs fused together as he kicked powerfully to propel himself through the water. His mind was becoming cloudier. His body, it seemed to him, was now snaking from side to side, raw power rippling through it.

Suddenly the moon, unable to watch anymore, hid behind a large cloud. As the world went dark, the group of sharks dived. As one, the six bodies dove into the inky depths of the waiting ocean.

On shore, no one witnessed the event. But a small owl, perched on top of Kiri's hut, saw, and its cries echoed out over the bay in mournful grief.

'Āmama, ua noa.

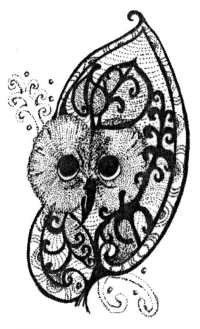

213

THE PROMISE KEPT

I don't know how we kept body and soul together as the intensity of the connection between Kiri and T'hane was played out through us over the weeks, but keep them together we did. We were somehow cocooned from all but the essentials of everyday reality until the whole story had emerged, then suddenly it was over. We were both struck by the enormity of what had taken place and the privilege of playing our part in fulfilling Kiri's promise to T'hane who for the first time, through Megan and I, was able to experience just how much he really loved her. It was amazing to us that this love had endured over a vast expanse of time and space and how important it was to Kiri that his promise to T'hane was kept. It felt to us as if we had in some way been instrumental in freeing these two souls. It was as if they could not move on until this promise had been fulfilled.

It had been about six months in all since the stuff with Kiri and T'hane really kicked in and then suddenly they were gone. Well, that's not strictly true. It felt like they moved away from us a bit so that we were still in contact, but their influence on our lives became less. The whole thing had been traumatic in the extreme. Both our lives had been effectively turned upside down and in the process we had lost many friends and family that couldn't understand what was going on with us, and we were not in a position to be able to explain to them. The whole thing seemed so unreal now that it was over and yet it had been so palpable, so absolutely real whilst it had been going on. We were both relatively shell shocked. It felt like we had survived a tornado. We had emerged physically unscathed but emotionally battered. There was also a very palpable feeling of loss as well. Kiri and T'hane were no longer a real part of us and they were missed. They still seemed to have the ability to channel information to us but it now had to come through the filter of our conscious minds instead of being given directly. It was true that we had been given an extraordinary experience of the power of Love. We had been emotionally and psychically opened up to an extreme degree and yet through it all, we had felt supported and sustained by these beings. We truly were taken to the edge on so many occasions and yet, in hind sight, we realized that we were never asked to do anything that we could not handle even though it did not always feel like it at the time. In fact, as the saying goes, 'that which does not kill you, makes you strong.' We had both found a tremendous strength and belief in true Love. Love that has nothing to do with personality or projection but which is at the very heart of each of us. That essential part of all of us that is a true reflection of the Divine. We had been exposed to the many possibilities of energy. Our minds had been stretched to encompass the impossible. In fact, if we could allow ourselves to get out of the way, the most amazing things could, and in fact, did occur. Things that often bordered on the miraculous.

It was also abundantly clear to us that throughout all of this we had been privy to the most amazing teaching. As much as Kiri wanted to fulfil his promise to T'hane he also wanted the ancient teaching, that was so much a part of him, shared. In this way he could once again find a state of balance, or pono, after the vengeful act that he perpetrated all those years ago. It took us a while to get the word out that we were offering this work but gradually we began to teach it and we were always surprised and delighted at the power of it to make real changes in peoples lives. We felt Kiri's presence and involvement whenever we came together with a group of people. The atmosphere in the room would become charged

216

and thick with the now familiar golden glow, spontaneous healings would occur, and often there would be an accompanying shift in the elements. One time a crack of thunder out of a clear sky, another time a swirl of dense fog on a clear evening. On one occasion, in the USA, a tiny crowd of chipmunks were attracted to the windows of the work room. Drawn by some unseen thread they stood on tip toes to get a glimpse inside the room. Megan commented that it was like magic but without Disney!

We even got a glimpse of a UFO on one occasion high up in the Scottish mountains. The work was certainly attracting attention! Those that we shared the techniques with, took them and shared them with others in turn and the magic of Kiri was taken out across the globe. After a while I decided to commit to audio tape everything that I had learned and subsequently come to understand. There was so much! My memory was good but I knew that I would not be able to hold on to all this indefinitely.

It seemed that we had been given a gift, but like all great gifts it was a two edged sword. The knowledge we now had could be put to great use, especially in the field of healing and soul connection, and yet it was not without its dangers. For a while at least, it had set us apart from those that we knew and loved, and that was indeed painful. On the other hand it had given us the opportunity to look at life through different eyes, and the friends that came our way afterwards were often extraordinary people. Many of them had had their own awakenings and spiritual journeys, and so there was a newfound resonance and a connection that went soul deep. For this we are grateful and appreciative.

We have come to realize that we exist through the grace and mercy of energies that we know little about at this moment in time. Energies that take us every which way and yet we both believe that, above all, we are loved and guided.

To our entrenched and stubborn minds it often feels like an onslaught when Life deals you a curve ball and you find yourself wrong-footed and seemingly ill prepared. It is in those moments that something extraordinary can occur if we only have the courage to let it unfold.

Kiri and T'hane had taught us many valuable lessons. Through their struggles, we learnt to recognize those same struggles in ourselves. As we let their story unfold through our lives, we too learnt many of their lessons and felt the same agony and ecstasy as them. To many their story sounds extremely sad, and yet never to know suffering is never to know joy. Like the swing of a pendulum, the depths of despair can suddenly give rise to the most exulted experience of Love.

Are we glad that all this happened to us? Yes! Would we want to go through a similar experience again? No! Nor do I think that we will be asked to do so. And yet in our everyday dealings with Life, as those differing energies are played out around us, we have to face the same decisions and challenges that we did through those days with Kiri. I would like to think that we deal with them in an easier fashion. That we resist less. However, it seems constant work to keep reminding ourselves to Trust. Trust that we are sent the challenges in life in order for us to grow strong and to learn and accept more about ourselves. Trust that we are indeed Divine beings in our own right and that we are supported and loved. Trust that as we open ourselves more and more to Life's wisdom and connect more and more to the Soul in every aspect of Creation, that we will find our true happiness and Love and be constantly blown away by it. Will we continue to work with the information that we were given? Will we share it with everyone and anyone who is open enough to learn from it? Will we keep reminding ourselves of the need to be conscious and aware and open? Will we honour the life process?

YES. WE PROMISE.

La‘a ka pae moku
hānau ia mai loko mai o ke ahi a i ka wai ola a Kāne
e maliu i nā kūpuna, i nā pōhaku
mai ke au lipolipo mai, ua pa‘a nō ka ‘ike ma lalo o ko kākou
meheu wāwae

E maliu i ko lākou mo‘olelo
ma ka la‘i ma waena o ka hū o ka makani
a me ka‘oē o ke kai Kāne
E ho‘ohanohano ‘ia lākou, he kahu mo‘olelo
mālama ‘ia no nā kūpuna
mālama ‘ia, he makana no kākou

La‘a ke kanaka
hānau ‘ia mai loko mai o ke ahi a i ka wai ola a Kāne
e maliu i nā kūpuna, i nā Akua
mai ke au lipolipo mai, ua pa‘a ka ‘ike ma loko lilo loa iho

E maliu i ka leo i lohe ‘ia
ma ke kio o ke koa‘e kea
a me ke kakani o ka nai‘a
e ho‘ohanohano ‘ia lākou, he ‘ohana
mālama ‘ia ka hō‘ihi i kekahi i kekahi
mālama ‘ia ke aloha, kā lākou makana no kākou

La‘a ka ‘uhane
hānau ‘ia mai loko mai o ka hui ‘ana, ka ho‘omanawanui, a me ka
pule
e maliu i kou makua, ‘o ka lā
e ho‘ohanohano ‘ia ke alo mālamalama o ka mahina, maluhia ka
pu‘uwai

E maliu i ka heahea
mai loko lilo loa o ka na‘au
mai ke po‘o a ka hi‘u
e ho‘ohanohano ‘ia ke ola mau
e mālama mau i kā ke Akua
e ho‘oku‘u aku i kou ‘uhane, ‘o kou makana nō ia i ke Akua lani

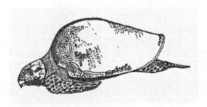

220

Sacred body of islands
Born of fire into the waters of life
Listen to your ancestors, the rocks.
Old as time, wisdom encapsulated beneath our feet.

Listen to the story that they tell
Hidden in the silence between the winds whistling
And the mighty oceans roar.
Honour them as the record keepers.
Held in trust for the ancestors
Held in trust, their gift for us.

Sacred body of man
Born of fire into the waters of life.
Listen to your ancestors, the gods
Old as time, wisdom encapsulated in your being.

Listen to the voice you hear
Hidden in the white birds cry
And the dolphins chirp.
Honour them as family.
Hold them in reverence for each other.
Hold them in love, their gift to us.
Sacred body of Spirit
Born of integration, diligence and prayer
Listen to your father the sun.
Honour the moons soft face, encapsulated in inner calm.

Listen to the insistent call
Hidden in the mantle of your soul
And woven into every stitch of your being.
Honour life's immortal thread.
Hold fast to the Great Source's plan.
Release your spirit. Your gift to the creator.

From
MasterWorks International

an in-depth look at the Kahuna teachings
from
A Promise Kept
entitled

The Power of Love
A Guide to Consciousness and Change

Due winter 2003

Printed in the United States
1321500005B/181-192